DRY BONES

Recent Titles by Margaret Mayhew from Severn House

A FOREIGN FIELD
DRY BONES
I'LL BE SEEING YOU
THE LAST WOLF
THE LITTLE SHIP
OLD SOLDIERS NEVER DIE
OUR YANKS
THE PATHFINDER
QUADRILLE
ROSEBUDS
THOSE IN PERIL
THREE SILENT THINGS

DRY BONES

A Village Mystery

Margaret Mayhew

Severn House Large Print
London & New York

This first large print edition published 2015
in Great Britain and the USA by
SEVERN HOUSE PUBLISHERS LTD of
19 Cedar Road, Sutton, Surrey, England, SM2 5DA.
First world regular print edition published 2012 by
Severn House Publishers Ltd., London and New York.

British Library Cataloguing in Publication Data

Mayhew, Margaret, 1936–author.
  Dry bones.
  1. Dorset (England)–Fiction. 2. Detective and mystery
  stories. 3. Large type books.
  I. Title
  823.9'14-dc23

  ISBN-13: 978-0-7278-7283-8

Typeset by Palimpsest Book Production Ltd.,
Falkirk, Stirlingshire, Scotland.

For Philip

One

In early spring, the Colonel went down with a bad attack of flu. Apart from a bout of malaria when he'd been serving out in the tropics, his health had always been remarkably good. There had been the usual childhood diseases – measles, chickenpox, mumps, and so on – but he could not remember any of them being as unpleasant as this, not even the malaria.

He lay aching and miserable in his bed at Pond Cottage – the only consolation being that the bedroom window overlooked Frog End village green and he could see the occasional passer-by to cheer his day. Major Cuthbertson, for instance, purposefully striding out in the direction of the Dog and Duck; Mrs Cuthbertson crouched balefully over the wheel of their Escort, bound for her ladies' bridge afternoon; Miss Butler emerging like a timid mouse from Lupin Cottage on the other side of the green; the nice young vicar chugging along in his battered saloon to make his calls; the organist, Miss Hartshorne, on her sit-up-and-beg bicycle, weaving her way towards the church; Philippa Rankin cantering one of her riding school ponies over the grass; Mrs Bentley out with her four dachshunds, their tangled leads encircling her stout legs like ribbons round a maypole.

Life was going on, just as normal, for everyone

1

else while he had been summarily removed from its orbit. He was an outsider: a germ-ridden pariah. Banished beyond the pale.

He turned his head towards the photograph of Laura on the bedside table beside him. There was another much grander studio portrait of her in the sitting room below, as well as the large silver-framed one taken at their wedding, but this simple snapshot was the image that he carried in his heart. He had taken it himself when they had been on honeymoon, many years ago. Laura was wearing a cotton frock, her hair blowing in the breeze and she was smiling at him. No glamorous gown, no studio artifice, no clever lighting, no tricks of the trade. Just Laura, as she had been and how he would always remember her.

If he felt low now with his dose of flu, how much worse must she have felt when she had been fighting her battle against cancer? He had seen her physical suffering plainly enough, but she had kept the rest hidden from him. He had never quite known whether she knew the truth. They had played a game of make-believe, encouraged by the jolly hospital nurses and the friendly young doctors, and it had been played to the very end when she had finally given up the unequal struggle. Let go of her frail grasp on life in the middle of one night when he had been at home in bed asleep and she had been alone.

He shifted his aching legs again and Thursday see-sawed up and down at the end of the bed, clinging on to the eiderdown with his claws. The old cat had given up waiting for the sitting room fire to be lit so that he could take up his usual place at the warm end of the sofa. He had finally made his arthritic way upstairs to the bedroom to settle firmly, instead, on the Colonel's feet. For a bony old moggy, long past his prime, he was surprisingly heavy but no amount of shifting and kicking would dislodge him. Nothing had dislodged him from Pond Cottage either.

He had been named by the former occupant of the cottage, an ancient pensioner, simply because he had first turned up on a Thursday. The stray cat had disappeared when the old man had died, only to reappear on the very day that the Colonel had moved in. Also, on a Thursday. It had seemed pointless to change it – as pointless as it had proved to try to persuade the battle-scarred, flea-ridden, torn-eared creature, to move on elsewhere. Thursday had graciously favoured the Colonel with his permanent presence and that had been that. There were times, he had to admit, when it was not entirely unwelcome; in fact, sometimes he was glad of it.

When Laura had died eleven years ago, he had found living on his own almost unbearable. The loneliness, the terrible silence, the long and empty days had come as a severe shock to him after a lifetime spent always with others. Family, boarding school, the army . . . always plenty of company and plenty of useful activity. Retirement and widowhood were uncharted and alien waters, something he had never even thought about or prepared for. There was still his daughter and his son, of course: Alison in her high-powered City job, Marcus with Susan and his two children resettled in Norfolk. They had both wanted him to live close by – either in a service flat in London near Alison, or in an easy-to-run bungalow down the road from Marcus and Susan. Instead, he had gone in stubborn search of a cottage that he and Laura had once seen many years ago when they had been touring on home leave in the West Country. They had stopped at a village pub and sat out on a bench in the sun. Laura had noticed the rose-covered cottage on the other side of the green and said that one day, when he had retired from the army and they had finally come back to live in England, they must find a home just like that. He had forgotten the name of the village but he had driven round and round Dorset lanes in pouring rain until, finally, he had come across the pub and the green and Laura's dream cottage. The roses were not in bloom and either distance had led enchantment to their eyes, or the inter-vening years had taken a severe toll on the house because it looked in bad shape. But, by a remark-able coincidence, it was for sale. Ignoring rising damp, rotting thatch, death-watch beetle, dirt and decay throughout, he had bought it, together with the half acre of surrounding jungle. He had bought it because of Laura and because he knew that she would have thoroughly approved.

His children, naturally, had not approved. Alison had thought he was making a bad finan-cial mistake and Marcus that he was losing his mind. They were probably both right. It had cost a small fortune to make the cottage habitable – to rethatch the roof, strip out hideous modern additions, uncover the ancient inglenook fire-place, expose beams, repair, replaster, repaint,

4

rewire, re-plumb, put in central heating and equip the kitchen.

And when it was finally ready and he had moved in, he had found the demons of loneliness lying in wait for him. It was easier to keep them at bay during the day, when he could get out and about, but when he sat alone in his wing-back tapestry chair by the fireside in the evening, whisky in hand, they came sidling forth to mock him.

He had been lucky, though, because help was at hand. The inhabitants of Frog End had gradually co-opted him into their lives. He had been made treasurer of the summer garden fête committee – a job passed on with alacrity by Major Cuthbertson, and which, naturally, nobody else had wanted. He had begun to meet people and to be asked to help out in other ways – cutting the churchyard grass, collecting for worthy charities, driving patients to and from hospital appointments in Dorchester, manning stalls at jumble sales, and so on.

The village might look about as lively as a stagnant pond, but beneath the surface there was plenty going on. For instance, there had been two murders within the space of a year which was somewhat unusual, to say the least. The much-disliked Lady Swynford of Frog End Manor, had been smothered with a pillow right in the middle of the summer fête, and a famous, if ageing, actress who had come to live in one of the new luxury flats at The Hall had been electrocuted in her bath on New Year's Eve. The Colonel had been caught up unwittingly in both cases, carried out his own private investigations and reached the truth.[1]

And, of course, nobody who lived next door to Naomi Grimshaw could ever feel completely alone. He remembered the first evening when she had appeared in his sitting room doorway, dressed in a purple tracksuit and white running shoes, her short grey hair bluntly trimmed like the new thatch on his roof. A self-styled widow, she had in reality been divorced from her husband many years before he had died. But, as she had shrewdly pointed out, widows and widowers were awarded far more sympathy and status points than divorcees. Especially widowers, like himself, who were always useful to make up the numbers.

Naomi had introduced him to gardening. *Something*, she had quite rightly said, must be done about the jungle surrounding his cottage. He had seen and admired the garden of her Pear Tree Cottage beyond the old stone wall that divided their properties. A place of natural beauty where plants seemed to have planted themselves, cascading and drifting as in some soft-focused Impressionist painting. No regimented beds, no garish hues, no sharp edges. He knew even less about gardening than he did about art, but he knew what he liked.

Encouraged and inspired, the Colonel had rolled up his shirt sleeves and Done Something. Jacob, the strong and simple-minded labourer from the Manor had been persuaded to help

1 See *Old Soldiers Never Die* and *Three Silent Things*

6

during his time off and, under Naomi's stick-waving, enthusiastic direction, the jungle had gradually been cleared. The stinging nettles and the weeds, the tangled brambles and the overgrown shrubs had been carted away, together with hundreds of rusty tin cans.

To start him off, Naomi had given him a lavender cutting and plants that she'd raised from seeds germinating on her cottage windowsills and in the lean-to greenhouse. She had also lent him several well-thumbed gardening books and told him to choose the rest himself so that it would be *his* garden – his own creation. He had never so much as lifted a trowel in his life and could scarcely tell a daisy from a daffodil, but he began to learn. He could never hope to emulate Naomi's enchanted plot but, by the end of the first year, his garden was making quiet progress and the pond which had been rediscovered in the great clear-out had attracted all kinds of residents and passing visitors – snails, newts, dragonflies, water beetles and boatmen, a grass snake, thirsty hedge-hogs and birds and even Thursday, who much preferred the pond or puddles to his nice clean water bowl in the kitchen. Most satisfactorily of all, given the name of the village, it had become home to a frog.

In the afternoon, the Colonel dozed until he became aware of heavy footsteps on the stairs and a slight shaking of the walls. A rap on the bedroom door and Naomi's face appeared round its edge.

'Come to make sure you're still alive, Hugh.'

The rest of her stomped into the room, radiating

health and vigour. Her puce-coloured tracksuit hurt his eyes; he closed them again.

'That's the spirit! You'll soon be up and about.'

Sickbed sympathy, he realized, was not Naomi's strong suit. She had probably never had a day's illness in her life.

He opened his eyes halfway and croaked, 'Nice of you to come, Naomi.'

'I've brought you something,' she told him and thrust the plastic bowl that she was carrying under his nose. 'Chicken soup. Jewish mothers always swear by it. Apparently it cures everything. I'll heat it up for you.'

'Not just now, thank you.'

'You must eat, Hugh. Build up your strength.'

'I will,' he promised. 'Later.'

'Not sure I trust you. Men are hopeless at looking after themselves. Useless at being ill. Cecil always thought he was dying.'

'Cecil?'

'My late husband. The one I divorced – remember. He went off with his secretary. I bet *she* didn't lift a finger when he was ill. Serve the old bugger right.' She glanced at the lump of black and tan fur at the end of the eiderdown. 'I see Thursday's managed to make himself comfortable, as usual. Do you want me to get rid of him for you?'

Thursday's eyes opened to gleaming slits.

'No, no. He's all right.'

'Of course, he is. He's a cat. They're always all right.' She looked down at him uncertainly. 'I must say you do look a bit ropey, Hugh. Shall I ask Tom to call?'

'Heavens, no.' He liked young Tom Harvey very much but doctors in general were best avoided. Doctors stood for illness and suffering and death, and for facing things you didn't want to face or even think about.

The grandfather clock's silvery chimes downstairs reached his ears. Six chimes. A Pavlovian call.

'Would you like a drink, Naomi?'

'I wouldn't say no.' She never did. 'How about you?'

'For once, I don't feel like it. You'll have to get it yourself, I'm afraid. Do you mind?'

'Not a bit.'

She knew where everything was – the whisky decanter on the silver tray in the sitting room, the glasses in the cupboard. No ice required and just a splash of tap water. She was back upstairs in no time and sitting in the bedroom chair, raising her glass.

'Cheers, Hugh. Hope you'll be feeling better soon.'

They had drunk many a glass of Chivas Regal together. An evening ritual begun when she had first called on him the day he had moved in. After a full and frank discussion of whatever was news or current gossip or of any interest at all, Naomi would return to her cottage and her two Jack Russell terriers and the Colonel, left alone with Thursday, would watch a television programme – if there was anything to watch – or listen to the radio or play his old Gilbert and Sullivan records.

He said croakily, 'I'm rather worried about the garden. Things will be getting out of hand.'

9

'Nothing that can't be dealt with, all in good time. I had a peek over the wall this morning and everything seems perfectly happy.'

'What about the lily of the valley?'

'Flowering away. Lucky you got the giant kind. The others always seem to get lost.'

He had done so at Naomi's particular suggestion but, generously, she hadn't reminded him of the fact.

'Any sign of the bluebells?'

'Lots of them. They'll all be coming out when you do.'

He said anxiously, 'The hellebores?'

They were one of his favourites. Bashful blooms that hung their heads and hid their delicate beauty. He had planted them near the kitchen door where they were under his eye and he could see them better. For all their shyness, they were one of the first plants of the year to brave the cold.

'Don't worry about them. They're tough as anything.'

Ruth Swynford – the daughter of the late and unlamented Lady Swynford – had given him the hellebore plants as a present and he treasured them. On her mother's unfortunate death, Ruth had inherited the Manor and stayed in Frog End instead of returning to work in London. With help and encouragement from Naomi, she had taken on the neglected Manor gardens, restoring them gradually to their former glory, as well as starting a small business selling plants. She had also become engaged to Tom Harvey, the local doctor, though not without a good deal of persuasion and patience on his part. Village gossip had it that Ruth had been having an affair with a married man in London for years.

He said, 'Any date set for the wedding yet?'

'Some time in the summer, Ruth says. She's being very cagey at the moment. I hope she's not going to duck out.'

Tom Harvey would almost certainly make an excellent husband, and they seemed to make a perfect young couple, but what if the magic ingredient necessary for a successful marriage was somehow lacking? Maybe Ruth was still in love with the married man in London?

'It would be a great shame if she did.'

'Not to mention a big disappointment in the village. They're all planning what to wear for the wedding. I saw Mrs Cuthbertson trying on a hat in Dorchester the other day – all pink tulle and feathers and the size of a dustbin lid.'

His imagination failed him. The major's wife's hats were usually the sensible country kind, made to withstand the elements and to stay in place in gale force winds.

'It could be just a small wedding.'

'No chance of that. Everybody will expect to be invited. Ruth's the squiress.'

'*Everybody*?'

'*Everybody*. And we haven't had a decent wedding in years so it'll be a good excuse to tog up. I hope you can still get into your morning suit, Hugh.'

'I doubt it.'

He had no idea even where it was – probably among the things he'd consigned to the cottage

11

loft. The last time he had worn morning dress had been at Marcus's and Susan's wedding, when Laura had still been alive. He could remember singing *Love Divine, all loves excelling* and praying to God that, for his son's sake, Susan wouldn't grow into anything resembling her mother.

'By the way, Naomi, there was something I wanted to ask you.'

'Fire away.'

'It's something I've been thinking about . . . but I wanted to ask your opinion first.'

'Well, spit it out, Hugh. I'm all ears.'

'Would you have any objection if I bought a garden shed – to go where the old privy was? I don't think you'd be able to see it from your side.'

'Of course I wouldn't object. Men seem to love sheds. I've never quite understood why, but I expect it's because it's somewhere to go and get away from women. Cecil always used to disappear for hours in his. He had rows of old jam jars on shelves, full of nails and nuts and bolts and screws. Dozens of spanners and hammers and saws and all the rest. I don't think he ever actually *used* any of them.'

There were times when he felt a sneaking sympathy for Naomi's late husband.

He said stiffly, 'As a matter of fact, I do need somewhere to put the garden tools and the lawnmower.'

She cackled at him. 'I was only teasing, Hugh. By all means, have your shed. Have you found one yet? Some of them are simply hideous – more like Swiss chalets.'

12

'There's a place outside Dorchester that makes and delivers sheds. All sizes and perfectly plain. It'll need putting together, of course.'

'Well, Jacob can do that for you. And he could start your sundowner terrace at the same time.'

The terrace had been Naomi's bright idea and the old flagstones that he had tracked down at the local reclamation place on her recommendation, had been stacked ready by the back door since early January.

'No rush.'

'Summer will be here before we know it.'

She would keep coming back to the subject again like a dog to a well-chewed bone. He wondered why on earth he had gone along with the idea in the first place. He slid a little further beneath the eiderdown and closed his eyes again. Naomi took the hint.

'Well, I'll be off, Hugh. Thanks for the drink. Hope you feel better soon.' At the door she delivered her parting shot. 'I'll put the chicken soup in your fridge. Be sure and have it soon. It'll do you good.'

He kept his eyes shut.

Tom Harvey called the next day. He let himself in at the front door which the Colonel had left unlocked and came upstairs.

'Naomi told me you're not feeling too well, Colonel. I've come to have a look at you, if you don't mind.'

'No need for that, Tom.'

'It won't take a moment. Flu can be a nasty thing. People think of it as a kind of bad cold,

13

but it's not like that at all. Specially as you get older. Better safe than sorry.'

He wondered how many GPs were left who still made house calls and took so much trouble. All in all, he thought, as the young doctor reached for his stethoscope, it would be a thousand pities if Ruth backed out. Both for her sake, and for the village.

'Well, your chest's clear, so that's a good sign, but I'd stay in bed for at least three or four more days, if I were you, Colonel. Then take it easy indoors for a while. Give yourself plenty of time to recover properly.'

'It was good of you to call.'

'Not a problem. By the way, Ruth sent a message. She'd have come round herself, but she didn't want to disturb you. She's got a favour to ask.'

'A favour? If there's anything at all I can do for her, I'd be only too happy. What is it?'

'She wants to know if you'd mind giving her away to me. At the wedding.'

For a moment he was speechless. Quite over-come. He cleared his throat, recovered his croaky voice.

'I'd be honoured. If she's sure she wants me.'

'She says she'd much sooner have you than anyone else she knows. Her father's dead, as you know, and there's only some old uncle left whom she hasn't seen for years.' Tom Harvey smiled down at him. 'So, can I tell her you're on for it?'

'Of course.'

'Looks like it's going to be the end of June, if that's OK with you.'

Naomi needn't have worried, he thought, sinking back on to the pillows when Tom had gone. And Mrs Cuthbertson would be able to sport her pink tulle dustbin lid.

He was deeply touched by Ruth's request. He was still virtually a stranger to the village, after all. Most of the inhabitants of Frog End had lived there for years, some of them for all their lives. This was indeed an honour.

Unfortunately, there didn't seem much hope that he would be called upon to give away his own daughter. If Alison ever did decide to get married – unlikely in her high-flying world – he couldn't imagine her going for a full-blown, traditional church wedding. This would be his one and only shot at the role and he hoped to God that he was worthy of it. The very first thing he'd do when he was up and about again would be to hunt for the morning suit.

Two

By the end of May, the Colonel was fully recovered from his flu.

The new garden shed was up, Jacob had levelled and prepared the ground for the sundowner terrace and the first flagstones were in place. With his shambling gait and furtive manner, the poor chap might look a bit strange but when it came to doing a thorough job of labour, Jacob was second to none. The Colonel knew that if he had tried to do either task himself, he would almost certainly have made a hash of things.

The front doorbell rang and when he went to answer it he found Freda Butler, from across the green, standing outside.

She said anxiously, 'I'm so sorry to trouble you, Colonel . . . so sorry.'

Poor little Miss Butler, he thought. Always anxious, always apologizing. She had been dealt a poor hand in life: bullied and despised by her late father, a fearsome Admiral of the Royal Navy, while she had followed a rather unsatisfactory career of her own in the WRENs. She had once, *in extremis*, confided in the Colonel – an occasion never referred to by either of them again.

He smiled at her reassuringly. 'It's quite all right, Miss Butler. Would you like to come in?'

Her cheeks went pink. 'Oh, no. I shouldn't dream of it . . . I'm sure you're very busy.'

Very busy were not words that generally applied to his normal day.

He said, 'Not at all. As a matter of fact, I was just going to make myself a cup of coffee. Will you join me?'

The pink went a shade deeper and he could see her wavering. 'I wouldn't want to put you to any trouble.'

'It's no trouble. Shall we be informal and go into the kitchen?'

She tiptoed after him down the hallway. 'If you're really sure . . .'

He filled the kettle and switched it on. 'Do you mind instant coffee? It'll be quicker. And probably better.'

'I wonder if I might have tea instead, Colonel? I very seldom drink coffee.'

'Of course. I'll just see if Jacob would like a cup, while we're at it.'

She looked round, apparently surprised. 'Oh, is Jacob here?'

He smiled to himself. Miss Butler would know very well that he was.

And she would know all about the shed and the sundowner terrace, too.

With the sitting room windows of Lupin Cottage in pole position on the village green, and aided by the U-boat commander's binoculars somehow acquired in wartime by her Admiral father, not very much escaped her notice. She would certainly have observed both the flagstones' and the shed's delivery.

'He's putting down my new terrace.'

'*Really?*' Miss Butler edged a little towards the

window for a better view. 'What a clever idea of yours.'

He didn't mention that the idea had been entirely Naomi's, put forward from her entirely selfish motive of quaffing his Chivas Regal in the evening sun.

'I have a new shed too.'

She peered out and feigned more surprise. 'So you have. It looks very nice. And how *useful.*'

He had already introduced the lawnmower to its new home, and hammered in a row of big nails for hanging the garden tools on the wall. He had also found himself sorting through all kinds of useful oddments and putting them in tins and screwtop jars and boxes in an orderly row along a shelf. After all, that was what a shed should be – full of things that he wasn't quite sure what he'd do with, but which would be bound to come in handy one day. He realized, with satisfaction, that there was room for quite a decent-sized workbench under the window. He could use it for doing odd jobs, mending things, even trying his hand at some woodwork, perhaps?

Jacob shook his head vehemently at the offer of tea or coffee, and the Colonel and Miss Butler sat at the kitchen table from where she would be able to observe progress with the flagstones.

'Is there anything I can do for you, Miss Butler?'

There must have been some good reason for her call. Naomi would happily barge in at any hour but not Miss Butler; she was far too shy.

The pink appeared again in her cheeks. 'My goodness, how stupid of me! I almost forgot. I

18

was wondering, you see . . . but, of course, you might not care for the thought at all . . . I'd ask Major Cuthbertson, only he's rather unreliable . . .'

'What thought?' he prompted gently.

The words came out in a breathless rush. 'Helping with our collection for *Help the Homeless.* House to house, you know. Like you so kindly did before, for *Save the Donkey.* They do such a wonderful job – soup kitchens, finding rooms in hostels, providing blankets and warm clothing. But, with you having been so poorly lately, I expect you'd much sooner not have the bother.'

'I'm fully recovered,' he said. 'And, of course, I'd be delighted to help. A very worthy cause.'

'Yes, it is, isn't it? There are so many poor people with nowhere to go. Living on the streets and sleeping in doorways and under arches. It's quite shocking to think of it happening in our country. Only the other day I saw a young man sitting on the pavement outside Boots in Dorchester, begging for money. It was very chilly and he didn't even have a coat. I felt so sorry for him and gave him a pound that I happened to have in my purse. Of course, when I mentioned it to Major Cuthbertson, he said it would only be spent on drugs.'

It was an opinion that the Colonel had frequently heard voiced.

'Just let me know when you want me to collect for you, Miss Butler, and I'll do my best.'

'Thank you so much, Colonel. It won't be until late June, so there's plenty of time.' She gave him a timid smile. 'You did so well for the donkeys. It will be most encouraging to have your support.' She sipped at her tea. 'Is this Earl Grey, by any chance? It tastes delicious. What a treat!'

He doubted if there were many treats in her life. Her naval pension wouldn't allow them. Come to that, his own army one didn't either and he was very fortunate to have some private income to supplement it. He could manage to afford such things as Earl Grey tea and Chivas Regal whisky.

They chatted politely for a few more minutes and then Miss Butler finished her tea and gave a final glance out of the window where the strong-armed Jacob was heaving another flagstone into place.

'I think it's going to look *very* nice, Colonel.'

'You must come and have another cup of tea with me when it's finished. If the weather's warm enough we'll be able to sit out there.'

She blushed again. 'How very kind.'

He escorted her to the front door and, as he opened it, she said rather archly, pulling on her gloves, 'A little bird told me that you will be giving dear Ruth away at her wedding, Colonel.'

'Yes, she asked me to do so.' He hadn't mentioned it to a soul but it was no surprise that the news had spread.

'I hear that Major Cuthbertson's just a teeny bit put out not to have been asked. But that would never do, of course. There's always the risk that he might overindulge. Whereas with you, Ruth will be in *very* safe hands.'

He thought wryly that while it was nice to be

20

thought of as so safe, it was also rather dull. How could they be so sure that he wouldn't turn up roaring drunk? Behave appallingly badly? Give an obscene speech? Presumably for the same strange reason that people were always confiding in him and trusting him implicitly with their deepest secrets. It was a mystery to him.

Miss Butler hesitated on the doorstep. 'I meant to ask if you happen to have any old clothes that you would care to donate to the *Help the Homeless* cause, Colonel. They would be most gratefully accepted.'

Most of his clothing was old – some of it going back thirty years or more – and the recipients' gratitude could be open to question.

'I'll see what I can find, Miss Butler.'

She eyed him uncertainly. 'Though, of course, with you being such a tall gentleman, there might be a problem.'

'I'm sure I have some things that might be useful.'

'And, apparently, toothpaste, shampoo and soap are always welcome – so they say.'

He was tempted to ask her gravely which particular brands were preferred, but it would be extremely unkind to tease her.

'I shall be happy to contribute some.'

'They mentioned disposable razor blades, too. I'm afraid I don't know much about those.'

'Don't worry, I'll take care of it.'

She thanked him profusely and scurried away.

'Hallo, Father. I'm ringing to see how you are?'

'I'm very well, thank you, Susan.'

21

He braced himself for a lecture from his daughter-in-law.

'You must take care not to overdo things after that horrid flu, you know.'

'I'm not overdoing anything,' he said mildly. 'I'm sitting down with the newspaper.'

'That's good. But are you eating properly?'

He moved the receiver a little further away from his ear. Susan's lectures were always delivered *fortissimo*. He longed to tell her, but never had, that he wasn't yet stone deaf.

'Rather.'

'And taking those multivitamins we sent?'

'Yes, of course.' The bottle was at the back of one of the kitchen cupboards. He had swallowed a few of the capsules which were the size of horse pills and then forgotten all about them.

'It's so important to have a good diet. Fresh fish and vegetables – no red meat and nothing fried or fatty. If we were closer, I could bring the right sort of meals round for you. Have you thought any more about moving up here, Father? Norwich is very nice, you know.'

He wished to heaven that she wouldn't always call him Father. Hugh would do so much better.

'No, I can't say I have.'

'There's a bungalow for sale just down the road. You could come and stay the night with us and view it. It's a very nice property.'

Why were houses for sale always properties and why did one always view them and not simply go and see them? It was estate agents' speak – like nestling and boasting and featuring. Never plain language and often downright

22

misleading. Pond Cottage had been described as having potential – which, translated, meant that it was extremely dilapidated and would cost a great deal of money to put right.

'Perhaps not just at the moment, Susan. I'm having some work done in the garden. I need to keep an eye on things here.'

'Oh? What sort of work?'

'A terrace at the back.'

'Goodness. That sounds expensive.'

'It's only a small terrace. It will get the afternoon and evening sun, so it should be rather nice to sit out there in the summer.'

Wiser not to mention the sundowner drinking part of it; Susan never touched alcohol and would certainly think it was bad for him. And better not to mention Naomi either. His daughter-in-law, who had never met his next-door neighbour, was always on the alert for predatory women who might ensnare him. He changed the subject smoothly.

'How are the children?'

'Eric has an awful cold and it's gone straight to his chest.'

'I'm very sorry to hear that.'

He genuinely was. Once he had found it hard to appreciate his overprotected five-year-old grandson who, Susan claimed, was delicate and sensitive. Then Eric had come to stay at Pond Cottage on his own while Susan had been in hospital with a threatened miscarriage, and a visit to the Bovington Tank Museum had formed a firm male bond between them.

'How about little Edith?' His granddaughter

23

was only two weeks old and he had yet to see her. She had been named after Susan's mother, with Laura as her second name. He hoped, for her sake, that she would take after Laura in looks.

'She's put on four pounds. And last night she slept for six hours. She's much easier than Eric was, thank goodness.'

'Well, I'm looking forward very much to meeting her. Perhaps you could come and stay when she's a little older.'

He could take Eric off to Bovington Museum again, if they could manage to slip their leashes.

'I don't think I could cope with the journey yet, Father. It would be easier if you came here. Then Marcus could take you to view properties for sale in the area.'

Women were the very devil about clinging to ideas, he thought. Nothing would shake them off. Bulldogs were feeble by comparison.

'How is Marcus, by the way?'

'Well, they keep him working all hours at the new job.'

'I hope he's enjoying it.'

'He doesn't really say much.'

At least it was a job. When Marcus had been made redundant, Susan had gone back to her mother in Essex, taking Eric. The marriage had been on the rocks but, fortunately, the job with the pasta company had turned up and things had been sorted out. Times were tough for young people. His own career in the army had been straightforward, by comparison. He'd been lucky.

Susan said, 'Of course, lots of people are eating

24

pasta these days. It's very good for you, Father. Very healthy. Did you know that?'

Personally, he hated the stuff. Slithering around on the plate, no real taste – unless you covered it with strong cheese or some horrible sauce.

Naomi agreed with him. She had taught him quite a lot about cooking, handing on her misspelled recipes: *Sheperd's Pie, Sosages and Mash, Choclate Moose, Rost Chicken.* Good, plain, no-nonsense English fare.

He went on talking to his daughter-in-law, enquiring politely about her parents and then drew the conversation to a close before Susan could think of something else that he ought to eat, do, or not do.

The terrace was finished by the end of the week. Jacob had done a first-rate job and the Colonel made certain that he was well rewarded.

He stood admiring the look of the old flagstones which had already settled in as though they had been there for centuries. There was no substitute for the real thing, he thought. Modern copies from a garden centre simply would not do, and they looked worse with age, not better. The only thing missing now was the sun going down, and some garden chairs to sit on. He'd ask Naomi's advice on where to look for those.

He issued a formal invitation by telephone for that evening and she arrived on the stroke of six o'clock to carry out a terrace inspection.

'It looks wonderful, Hugh. Wasn't I right about it? You'll need a few plants to soften it at the edges – a bit of aquilegia, alchemilla, some thyme – that sort of thing. I can let you have those.

They'll spread themselves around if they want to. A nice old pot or two with some annuals, perhaps, but don't overcrowd it.' She waved an arm expansively. 'The whole garden's looking good, in fact. And your shed's not bad, either. Nothing like a Swiss chalet, thank God. Can I see inside?'

'Not yet,' he said firmly. Not ever, if he had his way. He'd done the terrace for her, but he was blowed if she was going to invade his shed.

An Englishman's shed was his castle.

'I thought I might send for some white lavender plants, like yours – if you don't mind me copying you.'

'Not a scrap. I'll give you the name of the chap I got them from. They're jolly hard to find. They're called Edelweiss, though I can't imagine why. Lavender's got absolutely nothing to do with the Alps.'

It had begun to rain, so they retreated to the sitting room and he poured their drinks. She had some helpful ideas about where to find the garden chairs – the old-fashioned kind that would go with the flagstones.

'By the way,' he said. 'I'll be away over this weekend. Would you mind very much feeding Thursday for me?'

'If he'll let me.'

'I'll leave the kind of food he likes best. His bowl is on the floor near the door. It's marked DOG, but he doesn't seem to mind.'

'Well, he can't read, can he?'

'Not as far as I know. And there's one for water beside it.'

26

He had installed a cat flap in the back door so that Thursday could come and go as he pleased, though if it suited him better, the cat would still wait stubbornly for the door to be opened.

'Where are you off to, Hugh? Somewhere nice?'

Nobody in the village could go anywhere without their destination being made general knowledge. He had sneaked off to London by train a few times and discovered that the platform was kept under constant surveillance by the local KGB.

'Wiltshire. I've had a letter from an old friend of Laura's – they shared a flat together in London years ago. She's asked me to go and visit – though I'm not quite sure why. I haven't seen her since Laura's funeral. Her first husband died quite young and then she married some extremely rich city chap. I've never met him, but I imagine they move in pretty exalted circles.'

When he thought about it, the whole thing was rather odd, starting with Cornelia Heathcote's letter:

Dear Hugh,

I expect you will be surprised to hear from me out of the blue. I'm sorry to have been out of touch for so long and hope you are coping all right in your new home. It must be very hard for you without Laura. I know how much she meant to you. I miss her too. She was such a dear friend.

To be perfectly honest, I am writing

27

because I need your help. Something very horrible has happened and I don't know how to deal with it. But I know that you will be able to tell me what to do. There's nobody else I can trust. So, I should be so grateful if you would come and stay this weekend. Howard is away in Hong Kong at the moment, and no one else is staying, so we will be able to talk in private. Do please come on Friday evening, in time for dinner.

As you will see from the address above, we have moved to King's Mowbray in Wiltshire. The house is just a mile outside the village and you can't miss it.

He had been rather intrigued. What on earth could have happened in Cornelia's cosseted life that was so horrible? And why was he the only person she could trust?

'Don't forget the fête committee meeting next week,' Naomi reminded him as she drained her other half.

He *had* forgotten it. 'Oh dear.'

'It's a crashing bore, I agree, but at least we'll have Ruth there this year, instead of her bitch of a mother, and Marjorie's not a bad chairman. She'll keep things moving along as much as she can.'

He remembered last year's committee meeting at the Manor all too well. He had been a complete new boy – lumbered with the unwanted job of treasurer – and had listened for what had seemed like hours while detailed plans for the fête were discussed: ticket prices, trestle tables, raffle prizes, numbers of tea cups and saucers, the dread subject of the weather and provision for rain. The late and unlamented Lady Swynford had held court from a condescending distance, seated in a Hepplewhite chair with her ridiculously clipped poodle, Shoo-shoo, on her lap, a long silk scarf trailing theatrically from one of her red-nailed hands.

'Another one, Naomi?'

She seldom did, but he always asked.

'No, I must go. Maybe we can christen the terrace when you get back?'

'I'll look forward to it.'

'I suppose you'll want to do the bottle stall again, Roger?'

Major Cuthbertson wasn't sure he cared for his wife's tone. He rustled his newspaper. 'I'll do it, if nobody else wants the job.'

'I thought you might.'

Damned nuisance, actually, and not worth all the trouble, he thought irritably. Only ever one proper bottle of whisky in the whole lot. Perhaps a half of vodka, a quarter of brandy, some disgusting British sweet sherry and a few bottles of undrinkable home-made wine made from the most extraordinary things. Pea pods, he remembered from last year. *Pea pods,* for God's sake. There had been turnip wine, as well. He knew that you could make vodka out of potatoes but he'd never heard of using turnips. Otherwise, it was fizzy lemonade or American coca-cola or some health thing called Lucozade. People were too bloody mean these days to give anything worth winning. Not that he could be seen to win the whisky. Not the done thing at all. If he did, he'd have to give it up. Last year he'd won the half bottle of vodka fair and square, shutting his eyes when he'd put his hand inside the drum; but nobody had noticed and he'd been in desperate need of a pick-me-up after the way Ursula Swynford had spoken to him. He'd always thought she was pretty keen until then. No need for her to have been so rude. Plenty of other women noticed him. He still had most of his hair, and the grey was rather distinguished, and he'd kept his figure – more or less. What about all those film stars who were in their seventies, or even older? Women liked mature men.

Marjorie was still standing in the doorway, like a dog on guard. He wished she'd go off and do the lunch so that he could get in a quick one before they ate. It always helped the old digestion which wasn't what it used to be. Marjorie's cooking didn't help, of course. Not her fault. They'd always had servants to do it abroad. He turned a page of the newspaper and shook it.

'Was there anything else?'

'I ran into the Colonel this morning. I told him how pleased we were that he was going to be giving Ruth away.'

'Oh, yes.'

'He's the best man for the job.'

He turned another page. 'I'm sure he is.'

A pause. She said quite kindly, for her. 'You didn't think she'd ask *you*, did you, Roger?'

'Never crossed my mind.'

'A newcomer was a much better idea. Then nobody from the village could be offended, you see.'

She stumped off to the kitchen and the Major sat for a moment, seeing slowly.

The old girl was probably quite right. Clever of Ruth to do that. Pick a complete outsider, like the Colonel. Considerate of her. She wasn't anything like her late mother, thank God.

Marjorie was crashing around with pots and pans in the kitchen. Just time for a quick one, if he was sharp about it. He tiptoed over to the cocktail cabinet, given by the regiment when he'd retired. Damned decent of them, except for the fact that it played *Drink to me only with thine eyes* when you opened the lid and the old girl had ears like a bat. He'd learned to get the lid open, bottle out, lid shut, tot poured, bottle back, lid shut again with only a few tinkling notes played. Mark you, he'd had plenty of practice.

He was faster than ever this time; reactions like a man half his age, he thought, pleased. He sat down in his chair again and took a gulp from the glass. Things looked a bit rosier now.

Three

The Colonel drove over to Wiltshire in his old black Riley. He had bought the car in the Fifties and had kept it in a rented garage whenever he and Laura had been stationed abroad. He had never been tempted to exchange it for a newer and more up-to-date model. True, he had to wind the windows up and down by hand, there was no power steering, no convenient central locking system or air conditioning, and the heating was tricky, but the rest of it was perfectly satisfactory. He liked the car and he enjoyed driving it. What more could one ask?

He had seen from the road map that King's Mowbray lay in the middle of a large and sparsely populated area to the south of Salisbury Plain. The few scattered villages were linked by a maze of lanes that frequently petered out into dead ends.

It was not a part of England that he knew and it was very different from neighbouring Dorset. Wide open skies, switchback land rolling away into the distance, wind-bowed trees, flint-choked soil. Man had lived there for many thousands of years, back to prehistoric times. Ancient earth barrows remained where the dead had been buried, together with mysterious formations of standing stones, and evidence of inhabitation – axe heads, arrows, utensils, coins, jewellery.

He turned the Riley into a narrow lane that, with luck, would take him in the right direction. At the top of a rise, he stopped the car and got out. A dull, overcast sky, not a house in sight, no farm buildings, only the tumbledown remains of a flint stone wall. A group of gnarled and misshapen trees, the dark glint of water in a pond, ditches fenced with strands of wire, long feathery grasses flattened in the wind. A bleak landscape. Chunks of flint lay at his feet and he stooped to pick up one. Its outer casing was chalky white, the flint inside glassy grey. It weighed heavily in his palm, fitting snugly within his fingers. He rubbed his thumb along a razor-sharp edge: a grisly weapon.

For some reason, the place gave him a sense of unease, even of menace. He was not usually fanciful, but the feeling was very strong – a conviction that ghosts from the past were standing at his shoulder.

He chucked the flint stone away and got back into the car to follow the lane another mile before he stopped to refer to the map. In fact, he had to stop several more times. A signpost made no mention of King's Mowbray and a promising lane ended in a field. Eventually, he saw a woman walking a black Labrador. The village was straight ahead, she told him. The Heathcotes' house lay about half a mile on the other side and he couldn't miss it. Cornelia had said the same in her letter. The dog walker's comment had sounded sarcastic, he thought.

King's Mowbray turned out to be a fair-sized village, sheltered in a dip in the land and with attractive old houses built of flint stone. They were all very well maintained and would certainly be very expensive to buy. The village might be out of the way, but the main-line station was actually still near enough to commute to London. In estate agents' parlance, King's Mowbray would be described as nestling in peaceful Wiltshire countryside, the properties up for sale termed rare opportunities, the area deemed highly sought after. He passed a very pleasant looking pub – the Golden Pheasant – and a lovely old church, also built of flint. The village shop had replica blown glass windows and glossy white paintwork. He guessed that its stock would be carefully geared to discerning customers.

When he reached the Heathcotes' house outside the village he saw why Cornelia and the dog-walker had described it as unmissable.

The entrance to the drive was marked by a pair of attention-grabbing steel gates, the house name carved in bold letters on a slab of granite at the side. The long drive led to a large house of stone and slate and a great deal of glass.

As the Colonel parked his car discreetly in front of the house, a manservant appeared at the door and came forward to take his suitcase. He looked Asian – probably from the Philippines.

'Please to come in, sir.'

He took off his cap as he walked into an enormous and high-ceilinged room with plate glass windows. The vast expanse of polished wood flooring was interrupted occasionally by Scandinavian rugs, scattered like islands in an ocean. Three immense white sofas formed a horseshoe shape round a log-burning stove that was big enough to incinerate a body. Beyond them, he could see a dining table capable of seating at least twenty people.

'Hugh . . . how *wonderful* to see you!'

Cornelia was descending a circular steel staircase at the far end of the room. Round and round and round. He waited until she reached the bottom and came towards him.

Ten years since he had last seen her. If anything, she looked even younger. There was no doubt that very expensive clothes and make-up, hair cut and coloured by experts and, probably, the wielding of a plastic surgeon's knife, all helped the fight against time. As she stood on tiptoe to kiss him, he caught the sweet and costly scent of gardenias.

'It's good to see you, too, Cornelia. And looking more beautiful than ever.'

She smiled and touched his arm. 'You're not looking so bad yourself, Hugh. You always were divine. I used to envy Laura like anything.'

She was wearing what was clearly intended to be casual country dress: silk shirt, cord trousers, a blue cashmere cardigan draped across her shoulders, low-heeled brogues the colour of shiny conkers. He admired her beauty and elegance, but she held no physical attraction for him.

'Diego will show you to your room and then you must come and sit down and have a drink.'

He followed the manservant up the spiral staircase. Round and round and round. As he had expected, the bedroom was starkly simple: a plain wooden bed, striped covers and cushions, more

35

Scandinavian rugs on the floor, streamlined cupboards, an adjoining bathroom of chrome, polished black granite and mirrors. The bedroom window had a blind instead of curtains and overlooked the garden at the back of the house. A garden of disciplined borders, perfectly clipped box and yew, immaculate grass, and with a very large and unidentifiable marble sculpture taking centre stage.

When he came back down, Cornelia was settled in one of the white sofas. He found a way into the horseshoe and sat down opposite her. In spite of its dramatically good looks, the sofa was uncomfortable. The back was unreachable, the cushioning like a bouncy castle. Cornelia, he noticed, had solved the problem by kicking off her shoes and wedging herself in place. Not an option open to himself.

A glass coffee table stood between them. He noted a row of overlapping glossy magazines, a large white porcelain dish in the shape of a scallop shell that could carry a pocket Venus, and a heavy book entitled *Iconic Houses*. Its cover displayed a house built of gigantic blocks of concrete, assembled at different angles and peppered with small round windows, like portholes. Sprawled beneath the coffee table was an animal skin that had probably once belonged to a reindeer. Although it was June, the log-burning stove was flickering away discreetly behind its doors. At full bore, it could probably bring the whole house to sauna heat.

The manservant carried in a tray with drinks – a martini for Cornelia, a malt whisky for

36

himself. They raised their glasses to each other.

'What an amazing house,' he said politely. Which it was.

'It *is* rather wonderful isn't it? Hans Birger designed it, you know. The Danish architect. I expect you've heard of him.'

'I'm afraid not.' He thought wryly of the Frog End builders, Jim and Dave, who had done the necessary things to Pond Cottage.

'When we bought the place three years ago it was just an old farmhouse. Practically falling down and filthy dirty. You can't imagine.'

He could – all too well. His cottage had been similar.

Cornelia went on. 'The same family had lived in it for hundreds of years but they died out when the batty old grandmother finally dropped off her perch. Howard bought it for the land, of course – he liked the idea of asking friends down to shoot. Do you shoot, Hugh? I can't remember.'

'Not that kind of shooting.'

He'd been pretty good with a rifle in the army, but he'd never much cared for killing game.

Cornelia said, 'Actually, we had to demolish the whole house and start from scratch. Hans did absolutely everything for us – the house, the interior, the garden. We didn't have to do a thing. Did you notice the statue in the garden?'

'Yes, indeed.'

'It's by somebody terribly famous . . . I've forgotten his name. Hans got it for us. It's called *Redemption.*'

'I would never have guessed that.'

'It makes the garden, don't you think?'

'It's certainly very striking.'

He remembered reading in a newspaper gardening column, that a garden could never be an instant creation. You couldn't order one, no matter how much money you spent. You could buy all the ingredients – big trees and mature plants, splashing fountains and statues – but there was always the likelihood of it looking more like a film set than a real garden. There was, he thought, some truth in that.

'Of course, the local planning people objected to everything but luckily, Howard knew someone who helped things along for us. And, of course, Hans's ideas are all absolutely brilliant. No hall, you see. He says a hall is just a waste of space.'

The Colonel thought of the cramped passageway at Pond Cottage. 'I rather agree with him.'

'So do I. He calls this room the dramatic heart of the house. It redefines the concept of the contemporary Neo-Modernist home.'

'Really?'

'Hans doesn't believe in dining rooms either, so we eat in here. Actually, he wanted the kitchen to be a part of the room, too, but I drew the line at that. I'm hopeless at cooking, you see, so there wasn't much point. We have this fabulous Filipino couple, Diego and Perlita to look after things behind the scenes, as it were. And, there's a daily cleaning woman who comes down on her bike to take care of anything else that needs doing. We have a gardener, too.'

The rich were very different, he thought, but without envy. Their life was lived in a world where architects designed and built dream houses

38

for them, just the way they – or the architect – wanted, and servants did all the tedious work involved in looking after them.

'We kept the house in London, of course. Howard spends most of the week there, except when he's away abroad – which is constantly.'

Howard, he remembered, was a banker. Not the kind who sat behind a high street desk, but one who moved in the complex realms of world finance.

'You said he was in Hong Kong at the moment?'

'Yes. He won't be back for another two weeks, or more. I came down here because the builders are working on the barn. We're having it made into a sort of games room for Rory. We've already done a tennis court and a swimming pool, but I thought it would be fun for him to have some-where indoors where he can play table tennis and billiards when it's raining.'

It seemed perfectly normal to her that her son should be given every plaything that money could buy.

He said, hoping there was no trace of irony in his voice, 'A barn sounds ideal.'

'Of course, the planning permission was a complete nightmare again. Even worse than with the house. It's about five hundred years old and they'll hardly let us change a thing. Hans had some wonderful ideas but they wouldn't agree to any of them. The hayloft and the doors had to stay and they wouldn't let us put in any proper windows.'

So, the Danish architect had finally met his match.

The Colonel said, 'I haven't seen Rory since he was about two years old. How is he?'

'Well, he looks rather different now. He's seventeen, you know. Taller than Howard. *Very* good-looking, though I suppose I shouldn't say that about my own son.'

He could tell from the tone of her voice and her expression that her one and only child meant the world to her, and it wasn't surprising. There had been no children from the first marriage and none from her second until Cornelia had miraculously become pregnant in her early forties. He could remember how pleased Laura had been for her.

He smiled. 'Certainly, you should say it.' He looked round the room. 'Do you have a photograph of him?'

'Not here. Hans isn't very keen on what he calls clutter. It completely spoils the look, he says, and goes against the whole concept of the house. So, we keep it very simple.'

'Ah.'

She ran a finger round the rim of her glass. 'Rory's away at Harrow, Howard's old school. He's in his last term.'

He saw the shadow that crossed her face; the nest was almost empty, the fledgling all but flown. It was a familiar situation.

He said encouragingly, 'But I'm sure you'll still be seeing a great deal of him. This house must be a big attraction.'

'Actually, it's not very exciting for him here on his own. He brings friends to stay, of course, but it's rather dull for them in the country. That's why we're doing the games room.'

40

'I see,' he said, but he didn't. An only child himself, he had never found life dull. He had made his own entertainment.

The manservant, Diego, reappeared to announce that dinner was ready to be served. They exited the horseshoe and moved to the dining table – black glass this time and with black pod-shaped chairs. The Filipino brought in a vegetable soup, followed by a superb dish of chicken and rice.

'Perlita does all the cooking,' Cornelia told him. 'She's a marvel.'

'She certainly is.' He thought of his own hit-and-miss attempts in the kitchen.

Cornelia asked after Alison and Marcus and he told her about his two grandchildren. Then, they talked of Laura: the shared memories, the happy times long past. So far, Cornelia had made no reference to anything horrible happening. Apart from missing her son, which was perfectly natural for any mother, nothing else seemed to be wrong in her life. Her husband was away a good deal, but wives of very successful, high-flying businessmen must get used to that. Howard might well have a mistress or Cornelia might have taken a lover, but surely neither happening could be described as very horrible. Different words would apply.

He searched his mind for what he knew about Cornelia. Not much, he realized. Laura had always been fond of her and that was a good enough recommendation for him. If any help was needed, Laura would have wanted him to give it.

He had first met Cornelia at the flat off the Brompton Road that Laura had shared with her.

41

In those far off days, she had been a working girl – a secretary in an advertising company, if he remembered rightly, though he doubted that she had taken it very seriously. Parties, nightclubbing until dawn, weekends away in the country, holidays abroad, a steady stream of personable young men. She had got married to a barrister and Laura had been a bridesmaid at the very smart wedding in St Peter's, Eton Square. They had not seen a great deal of the couple during the following years beyond occasional dinners in London, when he and Laura had been home on leave, and a meeting in Singapore when Cornelia and John had been passing through on their way to Australia. As far as he was aware, it had been a happy marriage. Then John had died suddenly of a heart attack. Not surprisingly, given her looks, Cornelia had soon remarried and they had seen even less of her and nothing of her new husband. She had visited Laura in hospital with a magnificent bouquet of flowers, and she had come, alone, to the funeral. He remembered, too, that she had written him a very moving letter of condolence.

The manservant cleared the plates and produced a delectable passion fruit pavlova topped with spun sugar. He wondered if the Heathcotes ate this sort of thing every day.

They moved back to the sofas for brandies. It was high time, he thought for Cornelia to spill the beans. Tell him about the very horrible thing, whatever it was. Surely it couldn't be that bad?

He went over the possibilities. Marital problems? But she would surely choose a close friend,

42

or a skilled counsellor to consult. Legal trouble of some kind? But she would have access to the best legal advice available. Blackmail? A lawyer or the police could usually deal very efficiently with that.

He said, 'Cornelia, in your letter you were obviously very upset about something that has happened. Perhaps you'd like to talk about it?'

She shuddered and pressed her hands to her cheeks. 'It's awful, Hugh. Such a horrible thing . . . and I just don't know what to do.'

He waited while she gulped down some brandy.

'Is it something to do with Howard?'

'Not yet.'

'How do you mean?'

'He doesn't know about it yet.'

'Is it to do with your son?'

'In a way.'

This was going to turn into Twenty Questions, if he wasn't careful.

'I think you'd better tell me all about it, Cornelia.'

'You were the only person I could think of, Hugh. You were always so reliable, so *wise*.'

Here we go again, he thought, ruefully. Saddled with someone's trust and high expectations.

He said, 'I'll do my best to help, if I can.'

She hesitated. 'Would you mind if I had a cigarette?'

'Not a bit.'

She fumbled in her pocket and produced a crumpled pack of Players and a throwaway lighter. Hans Birger would definitely have classified them as clutter. Seeing how her hand was

43

shaking, the Colonel got up and took the lighter from her. He hadn't lit a woman's cigarette for years; it had become a gallant flourish from the past.

Although it hadn't shown before, Cornelia was clearly a bag of nerves. He wondered if she was on pills. If so, they weren't helping much.

'Take your time,' he said. 'There's no rush.'

She took a deep and desperate drag at the cigarette, another gulp at the brandy.

'I told you about the barn.'

'That you're turning it into a games room – yes.'

'The whole roof had to be redone and some of the beams replaced, so the builders have been working on that for months. When they'd finished it, they started on the floor. It was just hard earth, you see, and we wanted a proper floor put in. A wood one, and sprung, so it would be good for dancing, too.'

God knows what it would cost. He had no experience of sprung floors – only of ones full of dry rot.

'That sounds like an interesting idea.'

'There was no point spoiling the ship for a ha'p'orth of tar.'

'No, indeed.'

She drew hard on the cigarette again. 'So the workmen started to dig up the floor to lay the joists, or whatever they have to do for floors.'

'Yes?'

'And then their foreman, Ed, came to see me. He told me there was a problem and when I asked what it was, he said that when they were digging,

44

they'd found . . .' Another gulp of brandy. 'They'd found some bones.'

'Bones? What sort of bones?'

'A skeleton.'

'Of an animal?'

'No. Not an animal. Ed said it was a human skeleton. Skull, body, arms and legs . . . all joined together.' Cornelia shuddered. 'They'd come across it in the far corner, about a foot or so below the surface. They didn't move it, or anything, and Ed came at once to tell me.'

'Very sensible of him.'

'He wanted to know what I wanted him to do about it. I mean, whether I wanted him to inform the police, or whether I wanted him to just cover it up again. Leave it undisturbed. He explained, you see, that if he told the police then there would have to be an inquest and, if that happened, then the work on the barn could be delayed for weeks – months perhaps – while there was an investigation. There would be no hope of finishing the barn in time for the summer holidays.'

'Would that be so terrible?'

'Yes, it *would*. You don't understand, Hugh. This could be the last summer that Rory will spend here. Next year he'll want to go off abroad for his gap year, then after that it'll be university . . . If I can get the barn finished now, he'd be sure to ask his friends down and we'll be able to have a lovely summer together. His eighteenth birthday is in August and I'm planning a big party for him, with dancing in the barn. I've booked the caterers and a jazz band. It's all arranged. Now everything's being ruined.'

45

He said slowly, 'Let me get this straight, Cornelia. Your foreman is prepared to leave the skeleton where it is. To cover it up again and say nothing at all about it to anyone?'

'If that's what I decide. It's up to me, he says. Actually, Hugh, it seems quite reasonable to leave the wretched thing in peace, don't you think? And, of course, Ed wants to get on and finish the work and be paid for it. And I just want it to be finished for the party.'

He took a deep breath. 'When exactly did this happen, Cornelia?'

'Last Tuesday. The builders have gone off on another job at the moment but they'll be back on Monday to start on the barn again and I have to have my answer ready. I just don't know what to do.'

The tears that were brimming in her eyes over-flowed down her cheeks.

He said, 'Have you seen the skeleton yourself?'

Another shudder. 'Good God, no. Ed says the thing's probably been there for years and years – maybe centuries. He says it wouldn't be unusual in this part of the country. People were buried all over the place.'

The Colonel had comforted bereaved wives of his men in the army and a woman's tears always moved him – so long as they were genuine. Cornelia's were certainly genuine, even though they were misplaced. He found his handkerchief and passed it to her, giving her time to compose herself. The ash was falling off the end of her cigarette and she ground it out in the porcelain scallop shell and mopped at her eyes.

46

After a moment or two, he said firmly, 'I think you should phone Howard and tell him what's happened. That's the first thing to do.'

She looked at him in anguish. 'I couldn't possibly, Hugh. He's thousands of miles away and in the middle of negotiating an important deal worth millions. He'd be absolutely *furious*. Furious at my bothering him and furious about the skeleton. We had lots of setbacks building the house and he used to go crazy. When we finally moved in here, the heating didn't work properly and there was a leak in one of the bathrooms. Howard went berserk. He said that if anything else went wrong, he'd just get rid of the house at once. The skeleton would be absolutely the last straw.'

'Then let me ask you a question, Cornelia. If you decide to let the builders cover it up and build the floor over it, how will you feel about that – knowing it's still there?'

She gave another convulsive shudder, pressed his handkerchief to her mouth. 'I'd be terrified that it might haunt me. That I'd see it looking in at the windows, tapping at the glass, coming into the house, standing at the end of my bed . . . But I suppose I'd get over it. And it would be worth it to get the barn finished for Rory.'

He realized that she was blind to almost every other consideration and that what she really wanted was for him to tell her that it would be quite all right to leave the skeleton where it was.

'Do you want to hear my opinion?'

'That's why I asked you here, Hugh.'

'You must inform the police at once, Cornelia.

Anything else would be highly illegal as well as foolhardy. Even if the skeleton is covered up again, that's no guarantee of the workmen's silence, in which case you could find yourself in serious trouble. The bones may, or may not, be hundreds of years old, like your foreman thinks. We don't know whether it's a man or a woman, how old he or she was, when or how he or she died – from natural causes or otherwise. The law in England requires that all unexplained deaths are investigated by an inquest, a post-mortem and whatever other forensic tests may be necessary to establish the cause of death. I'm very sorry to add to your distress, but that's what you must do.' He paused. 'In your heart, you know that you must, Cornelia, don't you?'

Her head drooped. 'I suppose so.'

He said encouragingly, 'It may not be as drawn-out as you think. Forensic medicine is extremely advanced these days and it shouldn't take long to establish everything about the skeleton. If it's hundreds of years old, they'll soon find that out and then your builders will be able to carry on. Do you see?'

She lifted her head and stared at him. 'But what I don't see, Hugh, is what on earth it was doing in our barn in the first place.'

Four

In the morning, the Colonel walked over to the barn. It was beyond the formal gardens surrounding the house and, on the way, he passed a hard tennis court and a swimming pool, the water glittering blue in the sunshine. The ancient flint stone barn stood in what once must have been a working farmyard. According to Cornelia, there had also been an unsightly collection of shacks and sheds and piggeries which had all been removed. The barn was a fine testament to another age and he was glad that the Danish architect had been prevented from making any drastic changes. The big main doors were shut, but he found a small entrance at one end and stepped inside. When his eyes had adjusted, he could see up into the cavernous roof renovated by the builders. A tall wooden ladder led to the hayloft.

The men had been digging on the other side of the barn and a tarpaulin had been laid across one corner. He went over, pulled it aside and switched on the pocket torch he had brought with him from the Riley.

During his army career, he had seen many dead – the bodies of young soldiers and sometimes those of civilians caught in crossfire; once, a small girl clutching her doll. He had always found it tragic, often heartbreaking.

49

In this case, the circumstances were different. These were bones. Dry and fleshless bones without identity. He could look at them with complete detachment.

As the foreman had told Cornelia, the skeleton was lying about a foot below the surface. Flat on its back, the Colonel noted, with the skull grinning up at him; hands at its sides, legs out straight. A normal burial position. He crouched down and shone the torch closer, studying it closely. A few fibres were clinging to the bones that might have been the remains of clothing. No hair, but teeth all present and in perfect condition which indicated a young person. No other obvious clues that he could see, though a forensic expert would probably have been rubbing his, or her, hands. He touched nothing, straightened up again and stood looking at the skeleton.

Dem dry bones! Dem dry bones! Dem dry bones! Oh, hear the word of the Lord. The words came to him from somewhere. A Gospel song, he thought, about how your bones were all connected to each other:

The foot bone connected to the leg bone,
The leg bone connected to the knee bone,
The knee bone connected to the thigh bone,
The thigh bone connected to the back bone . . .

And so on.

There was a chorus, he remembered:

Dem bones, dem bones, gonna walk aroun'
Dem bones, dem bones, gonna walk aroun'

Dem bones, dem bones, gonna walk aroun'
Oh, hear the word of the Lord.

Or something like that. Cornelia wouldn't want to hear any of it, but she had nothing to fear. These bones weren't going to be walking around anywhere, any more.

He stood up again and drew the tarpaulin back in place. Turning away, his foot encountered a chunk of flint stone embedded in the earth. There were others, too, dotted around the floor. No surprise, considering that the barn was built of flint.

'You saw it?'

'Yes. It's as your foreman described and definitely human.

We must call the police, Cornelia. Now.'

She was still in her dressing gown and, without the meticulous make-up, she looked much closer to her real age.

'*Now*? Must we?'

'I'm afraid so. Would you like me to phone them for you?'

She nodded. 'You'll be here when they come?'

'Yes, of course. They'll ask you questions – bound to – but we'll rehearse what you're going to say.'

'What *am* I going to say, Hugh?'

'You're going to tell them the truth – not the whole truth perhaps but at least as much of it as is necessary. You'll say that the foreman reported what he had found last Tuesday and that work was stopped immediately on the barn. You'll say that you were extremely shocked and upset by the discovery and couldn't think straight. That your husband is away on the other side of the world on important business and couldn't be consulted and so you decided to contact me, an old friend, to ask for my help. When I arrived on Friday evening, you told me what had happened and I advised you to call the police, which we did this morning. If they ask why you didn't call them sooner, you can say that the foreman told you that, in his opinion, the skeleton had been there for a very long time. Obviously, you won't mention the idea of leaving it there.' He smiled at her reassuringly. 'Try not to worry, Cornelia. You're doing exactly the right thing now. The *only* thing.'

She went away to dress while he made the call and half an hour later, a police car came up the driveway to the house.

Detective Chief Inspector Rodgers was a short, grey-haired man, dressed in a baggy suit, a shirt with frayed cuffs and an acrylic tie. The very antithesis of the sharply dressed young DI Squibb of the Dorset Police whom the Colonel had encountered in Frog End. Detective Sergeant Collins who accompanied him was young and keen, looking about the room and obviously making mental notes.

Cornelia had reappeared wearing her country casuals, discreet make-up and a distressed expression. The Colonel, watching her politely inviting the policemen to sit down, offering tea or coffee, was fairly sure that she was going to get away with it. He drew up one of the dining chairs and positioned himself at a slight distance from the group – far enough not to seem interfering but close enough to give comfort and support to Cornelia.

The detective chief inspector cleared his throat and the sergeant took out a biro and a notebook. Both men looked uncomfortable on their white sofa – the older perched on its leading edge with his feet anchored to the reindeer skin, the younger sunk somewhere in the middle. The detective chief inspector placed stubby-fingered hands on his knees and took a deep breath, like a heavy sigh.

'Let's start at the beginning, shall we, Mrs Heathcote? I understand a human skeleton has been found on your premises?'

'That's right.' Cornelia was keeping her voice just above a whisper.

'Could you speak a little louder, please. Where exactly?'

The policeman looked and sounded weary, the Colonel thought, as though he'd done it all too many times and for too many years. Very close to retirement, probably. A tired workhorse ready to be put out to grass. He had not been at all ready for it himself, but, according to W.S. Gilbert, a policeman's lot was not a happy one.

'In our barn. We're having it converted to a games room for our son and the workmen found it when they were putting in flooring. Their foreman came and told me. Apparently, the bones were lying beneath the surface. In his opinion, they had been there for a long time.' Cornelia

53

closed her eyes for a moment. 'I haven't actually seen them myself.'

The sergeant had wriggled forward to the front of the sofa where he could rest his notebook more easily on his knee. His superior gave him a withering glance.

'And when did this discovery take place?'

'Last Tuesday.'

'*Tuesday?* Today is Saturday, Mrs Heathcote. Why did you delay so long before informing the police?'

She dabbed at the corners of her eyes with a handkerchief – her own, this time. The Colonel hoped that the tears would start to flow in earnest. It could only help.

'I was extremely shocked and upset . . . I couldn't think straight. My husband is away in Hong Kong on very important business and couldn't possibly be disturbed. I was alone here, except for our two Filipino servants, and I simply didn't know what to do. So I asked the Colonel to come and advise me. He's a very old friend.'

The detective chief inspector turned to look at him, and the Colonel could tell that he was debating just how friendly he and Cornelia were.

'And when did you arrive, sir?'

'Yesterday evening. I drove over from my home in Dorset. Mrs Heathcote told me about what had happened after I'd got here. She was, indeed, very shocked and upset – as you can see. I don't blame her, do you, Inspector? The circumstances are extremely unpleasant. I told her that, of course, we must call the police, but it was late in the evening by then and Mrs Heathcote was very tired, as well as upset. It seemed reasonable to wait for the morning and for me to take a look in the barn myself to verify the situation before making the call.'

'Which you did?'

'Which I did. The workmen had left the remains exactly as they found them and I could see that it was a complete human skeleton. I didn't touch or disturb anything, by the way.'

DCI Rodgers said grimly, 'Well, that's something. But I still find it very odd that you didn't call us last Tuesday, Mrs Heathcote, as soon as the foreman reported to you. A human skeleton had been discovered in most unusual and unexplained circumstances. People don't lie down and die and then cover themselves up with earth. And a barn is not a normal burial ground. Why didn't you call us at once?'

The Colonel intervened. 'As Mrs Heathcote has already said, she wasn't thinking straight. This whole episode has been very distressing for her.'

The detective chief inspector was looking unconvinced. He stared at Cornelia in silence for a moment.

'How long have you lived in this house, Mrs Heathcote?'

'Since last October. My husband actually bought the farm three years ago but we had to pull down the old house. It was completely uninhabitable.'

'And where did you live while this was being done?'

'In our house in London. In Kensington.'

'And do you have other residences?'

'We have a villa in the South of France. Oh,

55

and an apartment in Aspen – but we don't use it very much.'

'Aspen?'

'The ski resort in Colorado.'

'I see.' If he hadn't before, DCI Rodgers had now seen exactly what he was dealing with. 'So, until you bought this house, you weren't familiar with King's Mowbray?'

'We'd been here once before to stay with some friends who live in the village. Mr and Mrs Fellows. They happened to tell us about this property being up for sale. My husband was interested in the land for shooting. There's about three hundred acres.'

There was another short silence while this piece of information was digested, along with the several residences.

'You mentioned a son, Mrs Heathcote.'

'Yes. Rory.'

'How old is he?'

'Nearly eighteen. He's away at Harrow.'

The detective chief inspector nodded. He was evidently more familiar with famous English public schools than with famous American ski resorts.

'You said that your husband is away in Hong Kong on business. We may need to get in touch with him. Where is he staying?'

'At the Peninsula hotel. But he won't like being disturbed.'

'I'm afraid we can't help that, Mrs Heathcote.'

Cornelia dabbed at her eyes again. 'Will there have to be an inquest, or whatever it's called?'

'There is always a legal inquiry into any death when the cause is unknown or unnatural.'

56

'I don't see how anything can be found out from some old bones.'

'You'd be surprised what the experts can tell us these days.'

DCI Rodgers levered himself off the sofa. 'Sergeant Collins and I will take a look in your barn now. Perhaps the Colonel would be good enough to accompany us?'

As they left the house, a second police car came tearing down the driveway. What's all the rush, the Colonel wondered? The skeleton wasn't going anywhere.

He led the way to the barn and the uniformed occupants of the other car hurried after them. The tarpaulin was removed and, again, he shone his torch down on to the skeleton. The detective chief inspector began barking out instructions. Lamps were set up, a photographer began work, two policemen were taping off the area. A man in plain clothes arrived, carrying a doctor's bag. Rather too late for that, the Colonel thought.

He stood watching all the activity from the sidelines and presently Detective Chief Inspector Rodgers came over.

'We needn't keep you any longer, Colonel. Sergeant Collins will take your address and telephone number so we can get in touch. I take it you'll be going back to Dorset shortly?'

'Unless Mrs Heathcote still needs my help.'

'Hmm. Well, the remains will be removed for examination and we'll have some facts in due course.'

'You'll keep Mrs Heathcote informed? I know

she'll be glad to get the whole matter resolved as soon as possible.'

'These things can't be hurried just to suit the people involved, Colonel. Believe me, I'd be just as glad myself if they could. I've been in the force for more than thirty years and I've got to the stage when I like nice easy, open-and-shut cases, not riddles like this one. I haven't got the energy or the patience any more, to be honest.'

He wondered if the inspector had any plans for his retirement. Was he looking forward to spending his days playing golf, or gardening, or making models? Did he have a shed where he'd be able to pass happy hours on his own, no longer bothered by wearisome police cases?

When the Colonel returned to the house, he found Cornelia slumped on the sofa, smoking a cigarette. She lifted a tear-stained face.

'Why did this have to happen, Hugh? It's *so* unfair. The inquiry's going to take ages, I know it is, and everything's going to be ruined. I could kill that damned skeleton.'

There were times when no amount of money could help, he thought. When no magic wand could be waved to make things better. It was a hard lesson for the rich to learn. He sat down opposite her.

'I'm afraid there's nothing to be done, Cornelia – except wait for things to take their course. The police will be removing the skeleton, so that's some comfort for you, at least. You won't have to think about it being there any more. And DCI Rodgers will keep you informed. You've just got to be patient.'

'Supposing they start suspecting us of having something to do with it?'

'Us? You mean, you and I?'

'No, of course not. Nobody would ever suspect *you* of anything like that, Hugh. I meant Howard and I.'

'There's no earthly reason why they should. You had no idea the skeleton was there, had you?'

'Of course not. But the police always have suspects, don't they? They'll be back, asking more questions and not believing me. Hugh, you will stay, won't you? As long as you can? I really don't think I can face this on my own. I'm a hopeless mess, you see. I take all these pills – to calm me down in the day and make me sleep at night, but none of them seem to do anything.'

Most women could lean on their husbands in times of trouble, but, far from Howard being a prop, Cornelia seemed almost terrified of him. The Colonel felt sorry for her. He was also thinking of what Laura would want him to do. There was no reason for him to go back to Frog End immediately – only the village fête committee meeting which could manage perfectly well without him. In fact, the opportunity to miss it was almost too good to pass up. Thursday would probably not be amused by his prolonged absence, but was in no danger of starvation.

'Yes, of course I will. But, as I've said, you really don't need to worry.'

'Thank you, Hugh. You're so kind.'

He phoned Naomi.

'Do you think you could go on feeding Thursday for a while? There's been some trouble here.'

'What sort of trouble?' Naomi sounded intrigued.

He told her.

'So I ought to stay. Hold Cornelia's hand for a bit.'

'I bet she won't mind that.'

'She's a married woman.'

Naomi cackled. 'They're the worst. Watch out, Hugh.'

'How's Thursday?' he asked, ignoring the remark.

'Cross. When I let myself into the cottage, he comes and looks daggers at me and then stalks off. Still, he's eating the food.'

'There's plenty more in the cupboard.'

'Don't worry, I'll look after him.'

'The garden . . .'

'I'll water anything that needs it, and pull out a weed if I see one.'

'I've just remembered – I ordered six of those white lavender plants and they should be arriving very soon.'

'I'll field them for you. How long will you be away, do you think?'

'I'm not sure – a few more days, I imagine.'

'You'll miss the fête committee meeting, you realize that?'

'Yes, I know. Would you make my apologies, Naomi?'

'I'll tell them that you've been unavoidably detained by a skeleton and how sad and sorry you are.'

He smiled as he put down the receiver.

* * *

60

Cornelia retired to her room for an afternoon rest and the Colonel walked into the village to stretch his legs and buy a newspaper. Cornelia's magazines had their limitations if you weren't looking for a house to buy, or interested in taking a vicarious tour of grand interiors, or in reading articles on hunting, shooting or fishing and the like.

A proper old-fashioned bell jangled as he opened the door of the village shop. As he had expected, though, the stock was catering for its well-heeled customers. No rows of dusty tins, drums of custard powder or sacks of sprouting potatoes. Instead, vacuum-packed and frozen foods, jars of gourmet delights, all kinds of cheeses and pâtés, an impressive display of fresh fruit and vegetables and wonderful-looking bread, cakes and tarts. There was also a rack of very glossy magazines and, to his relief, some ordinary daily newspapers – even the one he preferred. As he approached the counter a woman came from the back of the shop. She was somewhere in her late forties, he judged – straight dark hair cropped short, square-jawed, thickset and wearing a spotless white overall.

'Can I help you?' Her speech was gruff, but polite.

'Just the newspaper, please.' He offered up a note apologetically and she gave him the change.

'Are you staying in the village, sir?'

'I'm visiting Mrs Heathcote. She's an old friend of my late wife's. I expect you know the house.'

'From the outside. There was an old farmhouse when we first came here, with an elderly lady living alone. I believe her son had worked the

61

farm but he was killed. We never saw her. I don't think she ever went out. It looks very different now.'

'Yes, it must do.'

'Mrs Heathcote comes in sometimes, but not her husband. I believe he spends a lot of time abroad on business.'

'So I understand.' The Colonel looked round the shop. 'You've certainly done a marvellous job here.'

She seemed pleased. 'It's taken time to get things the way we wanted.'

'Have you been in King's Mowbray long?'

'Nearly eight years. It was just an old village shop when we bought it. All right in its time, of course, but the residents today want more than that. We used to run a delicatessen in Battersea until we decided to move out to the country. There's always plenty of demand for quality if you choose the right location with the right customers.'

'I'm sure there is. Still, it must be pretty hard work.'

'We've never been afraid of that. I look after the shop and the business side of things and my partner makes the cakes and tarts, and bakes the breads. They're very popular.'

He admired the carrot cake, the sticky ginger-and-pear cake, the cream-filled éclairs, the chocolate brownies, the fruit tarts, the lavender focaccia bread.

'It all looks wonderful.'

'We always buy local produce wherever we can – Wiltshire honey, local ham and bacon, local

62

free-range eggs. And all our fruit and vegetables are fresh from local farms. Would you like to taste this cheese – it's a local product too?'

He was in the middle of sampling a very agreeable crumbly, blue-veined cheese when another woman came out from the back of the shop, carrying a tray of tarts. She could once have been lovely but her looks had faded, the features become blurred.

'This is my partner,' the other woman said. 'We were just talking about you, Alice.'

He walked back to the house, and was sitting reading the newspaper when Cornelia came down from her afternoon rest. He stood up politely.

'You found the shop all right, Hugh?'

'Easily. It's a remarkable place.'

'Run by our tame lesbians. Well, Vera does all the running and Alice does all the baking. They're devoted to each other. It's rather sweet. Is it too early for a drink, do you think?'

'It's never too early.'

Diego was summoned and a killer martini and stiff whisky appeared in a trice. He lit another cigarette for Cornelia.

She looked up at him gratefully. 'I don't know how I'd manage this horrible business without you, Hugh. I couldn't cope. You won't go until it's all sorted out, will you?'

'I'll stay as long as I can.'

He wondered, though, exactly how he was going to be able to help.

Five

The story of the skeleton's discovery had been reported prominently in the local press and, when the inquest opened, the public gallery in the coroner's court was packed with ghouls.

Cornelia, very pale and dressed in sober grey, was called to the witness stand and stated that she had had no knowledge of the skeleton's existence until the foreman had informed her of it. The foreman testified that his men had discovered the bones not far below the surface of the barn's earth floor.

The coroner made notes.

'Did your men disturb the skeleton in the process?'

'Hardly at all, sir. They weren't sure what it was at first, so they fetched me. I could see what looked like a human hand sticking out and we scraped off the earth bit by bit until we could see the rest. We were careful.'

The Colonel was called and gave an account of the part that he had played. No, he had not touched or moved the remains; he had merely called the police on Mrs Heathcote's behalf.

'You've known Mrs Heathcote for some time, I believe?'

'She was an old friend of my late wife.'

'And when this discovery was made, she asked you for help?'

'She was extremely distressed by what had happened. Her husband was away on business abroad and she felt unequal to handling the situation alone.'

After Detective Chief Inspector Rodgers had given his evidence, an expert medical witness was called. The human skeleton, he said, was that of a white woman of between nineteen and twenty years old.

'What evidence do you have in order to make that assumption, doctor?'

'The shape of the skull gives the race and the endocranial sutures indicate a fully-grown adult, as do the closing of the growth plates at the ends of the long bones and clavicle. And the patterns of tooth eruption and tooth wear enable us to narrow the age with accuracy. Also, recent studies have proved that cementum – the mineralised tissue that lines the surface of tooth roots – exhibits annual patterns of deposition. Since the skeleton was complete, height was, of course, easy to measure. She was five foot, seven inches tall.'

'Can you give an opinion on the cause of death?'

'The examination revealed a severe injury to the back of the skull which would have been caused by a heavy blow of some kind. We term this blunt force trauma and it would almost certainly have been fatal, though, without a fleshed body, it's difficult to be absolutely sure. X-rays have not revealed any fragmented metal or metal shavings so whatever inflicted the blow was not made of metal.'

'Could it have been accidental?'

'That's possible but, in my opinion, the injury was delivered by another person, using a sharp and heavy instrument and with great force – though this is conjecture.'

There was murmuring from the public gallery.

'And how long has the woman been dead?'

'No skin or soft tissue remain. Bones do not decay in the same way, but they are subject to weathering or scatter if left on the surface. If buried, as in this case, insects cannot get at a body, but micro-organisms can and the acidity of the soil will also have some effect on decomposition. A buried body will take between one and two years to become completely skeletalized. There was no hair remaining and human hair decays in ten to fifteen months, but there were still some fibres of clothing material clinging to the bones which have not yet been identified. Materials take anything from a few months to four years to decay, depending on the kind and on the conditions. Cotton and wool, for example, can rot away in under a year while rayon takes only six months. Remains were found close to the feet of shoes made of leather which enables us to be quite precise about how long ago this particular death took place. Leather takes more than four years to rot.'

'So what is your conclusion?'

'That death would have taken place between four and five years ago. We can be more specific after further tests have been carried out. The weight, features and any pathology of the deceased can be established. And the teeth and dental work

66

could provide a positive identification. The two front teeth in the upper jaw had been capped.'

There was louder murmuring from the public gallery, instantly quelled by the coroner. The inquest was adjourned pending further investigations.

Not hundreds of years ago, the Colonel thought grimly. Not even one hundred. Not even fifty. A mere four to five.

Howard Heathcote telephoned from Hong Kong in the evening. Cornelia took the call up in her bedroom and when she came downstairs, the Colonel could see from her face that the conversation had not gone well.

'The police have been in touch with him and, of course, he's absolutely livid about everything. He wants to sell the house at once. He said I was to get rid of it straight away. Put it into the agent's hands, move out and go back to London.'

Police tape still encircled the barn and police cars still came and went to what had now become a crime scene.

'Rather difficult to do that, Cornelia – just at the moment.'

'That's what I said to Howard. Of course, he wouldn't take any notice. Anyway he's not coming back yet. He says he's got to go on to Singapore at the end of the week, and then Sydney after that. I told him you were here and what a help you'd been. You will stay on, won't you, Hugh? It's worse than ever now. They think it's a murder, don't they? Somebody hit whoever she was on the head, and killed her on purpose.'

'It would seem so.'

'It's *awful*! Like a nightmare!'

'But whatever happened, it was long before you and Howard moved in here, Cornelia. You've got nothing to worry about.'

On the following morning, the Colonel walked again to the village to buy a newspaper. Was there anything more beautiful, he asked himself, than the English countryside with summer coming round the corner? He had seen a good deal of the world's countries and climates and, in his opinion, nothing could match England at this time – the incredible greenness and lushness and fresh new colour, seen with eyes jaded by a long, grey winter.

He found several residents in the shop. Gossip was gossip the world over, he reflected, scanning the shelves for his paper and listening to them talking. It made no difference whether you lived in a big city, in a jungle, on a remote island, up a mountain, or in an English village. Where two or three, or more, were gathered together, there would always be gossip. This was a quartet of women, all dressed in Cornelia's deliberately casual country style – almost a village uniform – and with the same smooth ash-blond hair, as though they all went to the same hairdresser in London. Naturally, they were discussing the mysterious skeleton.

'It must have been a stranger,' one of them said. 'She couldn't possibly have come from King's Mowbray.'

They all agreed. Such an idea was clearly unthinkable.

'Poor Cornelia. Frightfully bad luck having it happen practically on her doorstep – and with Howard away. As usual.'

'Well, I hear she's got some chap staying with her – an old friend who's been dragged in to cope with the situation. Keeping Cornelia sane.'

'*Really?* Who is he?'

'Retired army, I gather. A colonel. All very respectable. Rosemary saw him walking through the village. She says he's rather good-looking.'

'Lucky Cornelia!'

'Anyway, whoever the skeleton belongs to, it's nothing to do with King's Mowbray. Nobody's missing from the village. It must have been someone passing through. A hitch-hiker, most probably.'

'What was she doing in the barn, then? It's a long way from the road.'

There was no sign of Alice who was, presumably, busy with her baking, but her partner, Vera, was standing impassively behind the counter, listening to the gossipers. It was impossible to tell from her face what she was thinking, though the Colonel could guess. She catered superbly for her customers, but she didn't have to like them.

'I'm trying to remember,' one of the coven said. 'When exactly did the Heathcotes buy the farm?'

'About three years ago, I think,' another told her. 'They had the house rebuilt by that terribly well-known Danish architect and they didn't actually move into King's Mowbray until last autumn. So, they're well in the clear.'

A third said, 'Actually, I wouldn't quite say

that, Lois. They used to come to stay with the Fellows at weekends. I remember Oliver and I meeting them at a Sunday drinks, and that must have been at least five or six years ago. And we bumped into Howard a few times in the Golden Pheasant with Crispin, letting everyone know how wonderfully successful he was. Rather a nasty piece of work, I've always thought. And a *very* roving eye. Heaven knows what he gets up to when he's away. Still, I suppose, as long as Cornelia doesn't hear about it, it doesn't really matter. I mean, it's nothing unusual, is it?'

The Colonel had found the last remaining copy of his newspaper hiding behind a *Country Life* and moved towards the counter. The gossipers finally noticed him and fell silent. He smiled at Vera as he paid.

She said, 'Would you like me to order one in future for you, Colonel? They tend to get sold out.'

'It's kind of you but I'm not sure how long I'll be staying.'

'I could keep one by on a daily basis?'

'It's not necessary, but thank you all the same.'

He raised his cap politely to the coven as he passed and the bell jangled as he opened the door. When he glanced back, closing it, he could see the four of them still staring after him.

Retracing his steps, he took the opportunity to observe the villagers' well-kept gardens at close quarters. He noted a well head, complete with wooden bucket dangling on a chain, statuary and urns, benches and pergolas, stone sinks and sundials – the sort of things to be found in a

70

pricey reclamation yard, such as the one where he had bought the sundowner terrace flagstones.

One house, smaller than the rest, was rather different. Its window frames and guttering were in need of new paint but the front garden, free of any artful features, was much more to his liking. He stopped for a longer look at a yellow and white honeysuckle scrambling over a wall and a wonderful mix of flowers coming into bloom: foxgloves, delphiniums, peonies, poppies, marguerites, campanulas . . . all ones that he knew and recognized. His own front garden was very dull – a short path leading from the gate to the front door, old bricks laid on each side and no flower beds. Only the rambling rose planted beside the porch redeemed it. One of the old-fashioned, once-a-year, double-flowered kind. According to Naomi, its name was Albertine. Many years ago, when he and Laura had happened to stop at the Dog and Duck pub in Frog End while driving through Dorset, they had noticed the cottage across the green because of the mass of pink roses smothering its porch and walls. Little had he known, then, that it would one day become his home.

An elderly, grey-haired woman was kneeling on a pad, working away with a trowel, a tray of young plants beside her. Instead of the usual village uniform, she wore a shapeless tweed skirt and a plain blouse. When she saw him standing by the gate, she got to her feet, very agilely for her age.

'You must be the Colonel.'

He smiled pleasantly. 'Must I?'

'We don't get many strangers in King's Mowbray and you stick out like a sore thumb.'

'That sounds bad.'

'Not at all. You're different from the rest and, in my book, that's a good thing. I'm Miss Simmons, by the way. Ester Simmons.'

'I was admiring your garden,' he said.

'Well, you're the only one who does. Everyone else thinks it's a mess. Are you a gardener?'

'Not really. I have a garden, and I'm trying to learn.'

'I'm just putting in some tobacco plants.'

He looked at the neat rows in the tray. 'Did you raise them yourself?'

'I couldn't afford them otherwise. Garden centres charge ridiculous prices.'

Her window sills would be crammed with pots of seedlings, just like Naomi's, and there was probably a busy greenhouse at the back. Even a garden shed?

He said, 'I'm afraid I'm not much use at that sort of thing, but luckily I have a neighbour who is.'

He went on appreciating the garden – the happy mix of plants, cheek by jowl, and the lack of any particular order. There was a place for grand and elegant design, for parterres and topiary, but not in an English country garden.

He asked, 'Have you lived here long?'

'Almost fifty years. I used to be headmistress of the village school: in the good old days of Reading, Writing and Arithmetic. Nobody teaches the basics properly any more. You mustn't encourage pupils to read books or to write legibly or to do simple sums. That's out of date. The school's long since closed down, of course, and been converted to a fancy residence. No young children here any more, you see. I bought this house for a song and I've hung on to it ever since. People often ask me if I want to sell, but I always say no. They offer some enormous price and simply can't understand why I won't accept it.'

'Well, this is a lovely place to live.'

'It used to be. I'm not so sure if it is any more, but I might as well stay on now. How is Mrs Heathcote bearing up? It can't be pleasant to discover a corpse in your barn.'

'Not at all pleasant,' he agreed.

'I wonder who she was – the woman?'

He said, 'Could it have been somebody local, do you think?'

'Very unlikely, I'd say. It happened about five years ago, didn't it? People move in and out of the village all the time – they're always buying and selling – but I can't recall anybody going missing. We would have noticed. It's something of a mystery.'

'A B & B visitor?'

'There aren't any B & Bs in King's Mowbray, Colonel. It's not that sort of place.'

He saw what she meant. A bed and breakfast sign posted outside a gate would lower the tone.

'Well, I'm sure the police will identify her soon.'

'I doubt it. They're usually more interested in harassing motorists than in solving crimes these days.'

He raised his cap to her and went on his way. Nobody in the village, it seemed, had any ideas about the owner of the skeleton. Even the coven had failed to come up with any suggestions. All of which pointed to a stranger, passing through. Possibly a hitch-hiker. Except that King's Mowbray was too much off the beaten track for passing traffic and murdered hitch-hikers were generally found in a roadside ditch or in a nearby wood, not laid neatly in the corner of an inconveniently distant barn – as one of the coven had quite rightly pointed out. Dead bodies tended to be difficult and heavy to move. He could remember the leaden weight of a fallen comrade whom he had struggled to save from the line of enemy fire – as it happened, in vain.

He went on to thinking about the damage to the skeleton's skull described in court by the expert medical witness, which had indicated a mortal blow administered by a sharp and heavy object. Being strangled was surely the more likely fate of a hitch-hiker? Strangled and dumped out of a car or lorry. Cornelia had told him that the farm had previously been owned by a batty old woman and Vera had said that the woman never went out. The barn would have provided a perfect place for lovers to meet, unseen and undisturbed, especially illicit lovers. The more the Colonel thought about it, the more he was convinced that the dead woman had been local. But who was she? And who was her lover? In a village like King's Mowbray – come to that, in *any* village of *any* kind – someone must remember something. Five years wasn't so long ago, after all.

Six

He walked past what must have been Miss Simmons's former school house. The old belfry was in place on the roof, together with the bell, and the words *Boys* and *Girls* remained carved over the separate entrances, but he knew that the interior – desks and inkwells, blackboards and chalk, rows of child-high clothes pegs and lavatories smelling of Jeyes Fluid – would have made way for an ideal home out of the pages of a magazine.

He walked on to the church and opened the lychgate into the graveyard. Ancient headstones tottered at odd angles, lettering eroded by time and weather and obscured by moss and lichen. The Victorian ones were predictably gloomy – all weeping angels and black marble. The newer graves were relegated to what space remained. Not so many people were buried these days. Laura had specified cremation in her will and, though he had honoured her wish, there were times when he would have liked a grave to visit, a place to lay flowers and to feel near to her.

The heavy latch clicked loudly as he went into the church. The peace and the silence immediately enfolded him: the troublesome world shut out with the closing of the door. Twelfth century, he thought, looking round, and probably built on an original Saxon site. The Victorians might have

75

laid their dead outside but mercifully they had kept their hands off the interior. Stained glass windows, rood screen, choir stalls, pulpit, pews, font, all belonged to centuries past, including a fine carved tomb topped by a crusader lying in battle armour with his crossed feet resting on his dog. There were wall tablets dedicated to local worthies and the names of the village men who had died in both the First and Second World Wars – in the case of the First, five members of the same family. There was also a list of vicars reaching back to the earliest times when they had been referred to simply by one name: John, Roger, Robert, Thomas, William. As the Colonel left, he inspected the visitors' book, lying open on a side table. Nobody had written in it since last August when a couple from Eagle River, Wisconsin, USA, had recorded their appreciation. *We love your wonderful old English church.*

Where there was a village church, a pub was never far away. In this case, the Golden Pheasant lay immediately opposite and its door was open for business. The Colonel crossed the road and went inside.

Like the church, and unlike the Dog and Duck at Frog End, he saw to his relief that the inside had not been spoiled. The oak beams had been left intact, flagstones still covered the floor, the original bar counter had survived and the inglenook fireplace had a proper grate for real log fires, not imitation flames. But there was nothing shabby or neglected about the place. Everything was clean and brightly polished and the greeting from mine host behind the bar was all it should be. He was a young man who clearly knew his job and took a pride in it.

'Good morning, sir. What can I get you?'

They discussed the merits of the ales offered straight from the barrel and he settled on half a pint of a highly-recommended local brew. He was just lifting the mug, when another customer standing at the bar, approached.

'You must be Cornelia's Colonel.'

He put down the mug to shake the hand thrust out to him. 'I believe that's my description.'

'I'm Crispin Fellows. My wife, Susie, and I are old friends of the Heathcotes. I was at Harrow with Howard and we were both at Sandroyd before that, so we go back a pretty long way.'

'I'm afraid I've never met Howard.'

'I was best man at his first wedding – the one before Cornelia – and he was best man at my first.' He grinned. 'I'm on my third wife now – and, I hope, my last. What's your connection with Cornelia, old chap?'

Smooth was the word that best described him, the Colonel thought. Smooth hair, smoothly dressed in a Vyella check shirt, Harris tweed jacket and corduroy trousers. The male version of the village uniform. Not much would ruffle him. Certainly not the discovery of an inconvenient skeleton in his barn. The builders would have been told to cover it up again and get on with the job.

He said, 'She was a great friend of my late wife. I'm glad to be of any help I can.'

'She's not very good at managing things on her own, our Cornelia. Gorgeous woman, but totally impractical. She drives Howard crazy sometimes. And, of course, she's completely besotted by that son of hers. I don't know what's going to happen when Rory finally buggers off. She'll be lost without him. Personally, I think it was a mistake to set up camp out in the sticks, but Howard wanted to have some land so he could play at shooting. Lousy shot, but never mind. I told him about the farm when they were staying with us. The old woman who owned it had just died and it had come up for sale. He spent a small fortune on the new house.'

'A well-known Danish architect, I believe.'

'Those sort of people charge the earth. Personally, I can't stand all that modern stuff, but Howard and Cornelia seem to like it.'

'Did they often stay with you?'

'Fairly often. My wife, Susie, likes having people at weekends and I go with the flow, as it were. I took early retirement from my firm in the City. Absolutely pointless to give myself ulcers when I'd made more than enough to see us out in considerable comfort. We bought a jolly nice house here with stables and a fair acreage. I hunt and shoot and fish to my heart's content. I'm a happy man, Colonel.'

Why, he wondered, had Cornelia not told Inspector Rodgers that she and Howard knew King's Mowbray quite well? That they had stayed with the Fellows fairly often – not just once?

He said, 'I gather the woman who owned the farm was something of a recluse.'

'That's an understatement. Old Mother Holland never set foot outside the door for years. The place was a total tip. It was rather a shame that things finished up like that. The Hollands had farmed the place for generations – father to son, and all that. Then a father and son both died within a year of each other and the grandson inherited at nineteen and made an utter balls-up of running it. In the end, he was killed when his tractor overturned – easy thing to happen if you're careless. After that, only the old girl was left and she'd lost the plot completely, poor soul. When's Howard due back, by the way?'

'Not for a while. Apparently, he has to go to Singapore and then on to Sydney.'

'Ah. Well, I don't blame him for staying out of it. Police snooping around, asking us all damn silly questions. They don't seem to have a clue whose body it was, do they?'

'I haven't heard any news.'

'They seem to think that somebody bashed whoever it was over the head. But it's quite obviously nothing to do with the Heathcotes, so Cornelia can stop panicking. They'd never been near the place until they bought the farm and, according to the papers, the corpse had been in the barn for four or five years.'

'I wonder if the dead woman could have been local?'

'Hardly. We're all highly respectable residents here,' Crispin Fellows said drily. 'Nothing disturbing is allowed to happen without our unanimous consent and approval. She must have been an outsider.'

Outsider was an interesting word to use, the Colonel thought. Stranger had an altogether different meaning. A stranger was an unknown person, whereas an outsider could be known but not belong.

He said, 'I live in a village myself. Not much passes unnoticed there either.'

'Do you have a decent pub?'

'It's been rather spoiled, unfortunately. Done over and overdone, if you understand me.'

'Only too well, old chap. Hideous carpeting, no draught beer, microwaved food, piped music, quiz nights . . . it's happening all over the country. We're bloody lucky with our present landlord. When the previous one sold up a couple of years back we thought it would be all-change for the worse but everything Kevin's done has been for the better. The place rather needed a new broom – it was time poor old Roy retired. His health was on the skids and he couldn't cope any more. His wife, Maureen, had some sort of chronic kidney trouble. She was pretty much an invalid, in fact. They retired to Poole and he died soon after, I believe. Hell of a job, running a pub. I wouldn't do it for anything, would you?' Crispin Fellows drained his glass. 'I ought to be getting back. Lunch calls. You must come and have a bite with us if you're going to be around for a while, Colonel. Susie's a hell of a good cook.'

The Colonel ordered another half of the excellent local brew. The young landlord had been replaced at the bar by a plump, middle-aged woman who was equally competent. A motherly type with permed hair and sensible clothes. He watched her fill the glass with a deft precision that must have come from long practice.

'There you are, sir.'

The mug was set in front of him without a drop being spilled.

She went away and busied herself polishing glasses for a moment before returning.

'I couldn't help hearing you and Mr Fellows talking about that skeleton found in Mr and Mrs Heathcote's barn, sir. What a thing to happen! It gave me the creeps when I heard about it. I've only just come back from a week's holiday, so I missed the police coming round. Not that I could've told them anything. I've worked at the Golden Pheasant for nearly twelve years and we've never had anything like this in the village. It's a very quiet place. Very quiet indeed.'

No village was that quiet, the Colonel reminded himself. Beneath the mill pond surface there was always a hidden and seething maelstrom of emotions and longings and secrets.

'Rather a shock for everyone,' he said sympathetically.

'The police don't know who she was, do they?'

'No, I don't believe there has been an identification, as yet.'

'Four or five years ago . . . that's when they think it happened, isn't that so? I read it in the local newspaper.' She gave the spotless counter an unnecessary wipe. 'When I heard Mr Fellows saying to you that the skeleton must have belonged to an outsider, I just wondered to myself why nobody's thought of Gunilla? Why she's never been mentioned? Not by anyone.'

'Gunilla?'

'The Swedish girl who came to work in the

81

pub a few years ago. She was here for several months. She'd come over to learn English and Mr Barton, the landlord then, employed her as a waitress – serving the bar snacks and waiting at tables in the dining room. She helped behind the bar, too, sometimes but she wasn't much use at that. The only thing she was good at was flirting with the gentlemen customers. She did that a lot and, of course, they all lapped it up, being what they are.'

He smiled to himself. As with valets, few men were heroes to barmaids. 'Was she pretty?'

'Beautiful, more like. Tall, slim, very long blond hair, blue eyes, and ever such white teeth. But she was bone lazy and, in the end, Mr Barton gave her the sack and told her to get out. She packed her suitcase and left.'

'Did she live in the pub?'

'That's right. There's a room up in the attics. It's a very nice room with a lovely view. She was lucky to have it.'

'Where did she go when she left?'

'Back to Sweden, as far as I know. Of course, she might have gone to London. She always said being in the country bored her.'

He said, 'Can you remember when this happened?'

She frowned, thinking. 'It would have been in October. I know that because we'd started lighting the fire. She was supposed to keep putting the logs on but she'd forget and let it go out. It was the final straw for Mr Barton.'

'Which October would this have been?'

'Well, my grandson was born that same month,

and he's four years and seven months now. So, it will be five years ago this coming October.'

Five years.

'Did she say goodbye to you?'

'No. I was off work the day she went – helping my daughter with the new baby.'

'Do you happen to know how she left? By bus? In a taxi?'

'There're no buses going through King's Mowbray, sir. Everybody's got cars – or bikes, if you're like me.'

'It's a long walk to anywhere, carrying a suitcase.'

'Maybe she got a lift. Or phoned for a taxi. You can do that, though it costs a bit.'

'What was her surname?'

'Gunilla Bjork. She told me she came from a place called Uppsala. I don't know exactly where that is.'

'How old would she have been?'

The barmaid shrugged. 'About eighteen or nineteen, I suppose. Perhaps a bit older. Hard to say with a girl like that. Always made-up to the eyes. Mind you, the hair was real enough.' She stared at the Colonel, looking upset. 'It could be Gunilla, couldn't it, sir? It's possible.'

He said, 'I've no idea, but if the police don't know about her, they ought to be informed at once.'

Seven

The Colonel telephoned Detective Chief Inspector Rodgers as soon as he returned to the house. He relayed his conversation with the barmaid at the Golden Pheasant, whose name, he had learned, was Betty Turner. The inspector, it transpired, knew nothing whatever of Gunilla Bjork. Not one of the villagers interviewed by the police had mentioned her.

'Rather odd, Inspector?'

'Not really, Colonel. People forget what happened last week, let alone four or five years ago. And if she was a Swedish bombshell then most of the men would deny remembering her at all. We'll have a word with Mrs Turner. Perhaps she can throw more light on the girl. And the previous landlord and his wife should be able to tell us something.'

'Apparently, they retired to live in Poole and he's died since. His wife's still alive but I gather she's in poor health.'

'Well, so long as she's breathing, she'll have some information of some kind. Thank you for your help, Colonel.'

Cornelia had come in from the terrace and sat down on a sofa. 'What was all that about, Hugh?'

'I've just been speaking to Detective Chief Inspector Rodgers.'

84

'What about? You're looking very grim, whatever it was.'

'I stopped at the Golden Pheasant on my way back from the village. The barmaid told me that there was a Swedish girl who worked there for a while about five years ago – just around the time the dead woman would have been buried in the barn.'

'I'd sooner not talk about it, Hugh. If you don't mind.'

'The thing is that nobody in the village has mentioned this girl to the police. Nobody. Don't you think that's rather strange?'

Cornelia echoed DCI Rodgers. 'Not specially.'

He was standing behind the sofa where she was sitting. She had picked up a copy of *The Field* and was engrossed in an article devoted to magnificently engraved and extremely expensive guns. As far as he was aware, Cornelia had never touched a firearm in her life and had no interest whatsoever in shooting.

He said, 'I also met Crispin Fellows in the bar.'

'He's a permanent fixture.'

'He said that he was the one who told you about this place being for sale.'

'Yes, I already told the inspector that. We happened to be staying with the Fellows.'

'In fact, he says that you stayed with them quite often – not just once. Is that so?'

'You're beginning to sound like the inspector, Hugh. We may have stayed a few times . . . I really don't know how many.'

'And I expect you went to the Golden Pheasant with the Fellows?'

'Once or twice. I'm not very keen on pubs, myself, and I hate beer. Howard loves it, though. He always raves about the local brew they serve there.'

'So, you might have seen the Swedish girl – when she was working there?'

'I can't say that I remember her.'

'She was very striking, apparently. Blond hair, blue eyes, tall.'

'Well, all Swedes are, aren't they?'

He persisted, 'It's rather unusual to find one working in an English village pub in the middle of nowhere. Are you sure you can't remember her, Cornelia?'

She said firmly, 'No, I don't remember noticing any Swedish girl at all.'

She was lying, he knew, but it could be for a number of innocent reasons, the most likely being that Howard, like the other men at the bar, had noticed Gunilla Bjork too much.

He said, 'Did Rory ever stay at the Fellows' with you?'

She lifted her head sharply. 'Rory has got nothing whatever to do with all this.'

'No, of course not. But did he?'

'He was away at Harrow.'

'Did he stay there in the school holidays perhaps?'

'He might have done once – I really can't remember.'

Another lie, he thought. She would remember everything about her beloved son.

'Does he know about the skeleton?'

'Of course he doesn't.'

'I thought perhaps you might have mentioned it in a letter? Sent him a news cutting?'

'Certainly not. He's got important exams coming up. I don't want him worried.'

She was like a lioness protecting her cub. Though the cub, he thought, was much more likely to be intrigued than worried. A skeleton discovered in the family barn would be considered pretty 'cool' by teenage standards. He did some mental arithmetic. Rory would be eighteen in August. When Gunilla had been murdered, he would have been thirteen. Surely far too young to have been of any interest to her?

She had done her flirting with the customers at the bar – the older men.

Cornelia had abandoned the pretence of the magazine and was looking up at him anxiously.

'You will stay longer, Hugh, won't you? Diego will see to all your laundry and get you anything you need.'

To be honest with himself, he was intrigued by the mystery, as well as mindful of his duty to Laura's old friend.

'Yes, of course.'

On Sunday, the Colonel escorted an unwilling Cornelia to Matins at the church.

'Everyone will stare at me.'

'All the more reason to put in an appearance. If you don't, they may think you've got something to hide.'

'How could I have? It's ridiculous.'

The service was well attended and the congregation had taken care to dress for their part.

Formal clothing rather than the country casual, with suits and old school ties, frocks, a sprinkling of hats and even gloves. It was a remarkable change from the modern 'anything goes' church wear of jeans, sandals and T-shirts.

They waded through the *Te Deum* and the *Benedictus*, confessed their sins, listened to the lessons, recited the Creed, prayed for the Queen and the Royal Family, and sang the hymns, including one of his favourites: *Judge eternal, throned in splendour, Lord of Lords and King of Kings.*

None of it meant much to him any more – not since Laura's terrible suffering and death. He sang or spoke the words when required, knelt down, stood up and sat down, all automatically. The rector looked a decent old chap, creaking his way up the pulpit stairs, but his sermon was uninspiring from its opening sentence. The Colonel's mind drifted away.

He thought about Gunilla Bjork. If she had been the blond bombshell, so-described by the inspector, she could have stirred up considerable trouble in the village. As Betty Turner had observed, the men in the Golden Pheasant had all had their tongues hanging out, and the barmaid had spoken of the girl as more than merely pretty: she had been beautiful, a word not so widely used. He had never been to Sweden and only encountered a few Swedish people. He knew almost nothing about them beyond saunas and *smorgasbord,* meatballs, dark forests, Volvos and Ikea, and, of course, *au pairs* who were frequently the subject of elbow-nudging jokes. Uppsala, he was aware, was a large university city, not far from Stockholm. For all he knew, Gunilla Bjork had returned there safely and was, by now, happily married with a brood of blond children. But, somehow, he didn't think so.

The service was drawing to a close. The collection plate had gone round, passed smoothly from hand to hand along the pews and borne away piled high with crisp bank notes. Not a humble coin to be seen.

Go forth into the world in peace; be of good courage; hold fast that which is good; render to no man evil for evil; strengthen the faint-hearted; support the weak; help the afflicted . . . Another of his favourites: a blessing that had something constructive, as well as instructive, to say.

They walked out, shaking hands with the rector at the south door and gathering outside in the sunshine. As the Colonel had expected, people were staring at Cornelia – openly curious stares and a few of them speculative. Skeletons, after all, were normally buried safely out of sight in the village churchyard. The sudden appearance of one in a resident's barn was somewhat irregular. Not to say unfortunate. Property prices could be affected.

Crispin Fellows came up with his wife, Susie. She had dark curly hair, rather than the usual ash-blond, and a warm smile. An invitation was extended for pre-lunch drinks.

'Do come back to our place. We've got a few people popping in on their way home.'

The few turned out to be at least thirty and Crispin Fellows had a lethal hand with a bottle.

89

The Colonel almost choked on his gin and tonic as he looked around the drawing room. The furnishings were deceptive. They seemed faded and worn in an English country way, but he suspected that they had been designed at considerable expense to give that impression. The antique furniture, however, was genuine.

The other drinkers obviously knew each other well. Mainly bankers and lawyers and senior City men, he guessed. There was only one regimental tie and he was introduced to its wearer – a Brigadier Lawrence who had served out in the Far East many years ago. They talked about Malaya for a while – the brigadier with morose nostalgia.

'Damned hard to settle down in the Old Country, don't you find? All rather dull by comparison. Phyllis has taken to it like a duck to water, though.'

He indicated his wife who was standing near by, engaged in loud conversation. The Colonel smiled to himself. She bore more than a passing resemblance to Major Cuthbertson's wife, Marjorie, whose prow would take to water as easily as any duck.

Susie Fellows appeared and took his arm.

'You don't mind if I kidnap the Colonel for a moment, do you Brigadier?'

She steered him away into a corner of the room.

'I've been dying to ask you about the skeleton, Colonel. Any news from the police?'

'I'm afraid not.'

'Betty Turner at the pub has been telling people that it might be the Swedish girl who was here years ago. She says she told you about her and that you were going to pass it on to the police. It's all round the village.'

It would be. Faster than a forest fire.

'Do you remember her?'

'Gunilla? Nobody could forget her. She was a knockout. There wasn't a man in King's Mowbray who didn't lust after her – even past-it old boys like the Brigadier – or a woman who didn't want to scratch her eyes out – myself included. Not that she was Crispin's type; he doesn't like it thrust at him and Gunilla did plenty of thrusting in all directions.'

'Nobody mentioned her to the police.'

'Well, to paraphrase the immortal response of Mandy Rice-Davies to the judge, they wouldn't, would they? And, anyway, everyone had assumed that she'd buzzed off back to Sweden.'

Not all of you, he thought. One of you knew that she hadn't.

He said, 'Cornelia doesn't seem to remember her at all – but then she and Howard hadn't moved into King's Mowbray at that time.'

'Oh, she'll remember her all right, Colonel. We used to take Cornelia and Howard to the Golden Pheasant for dinner sometimes when they came to stay. Gunilla would be there with her short skirts and her cleavage, tossing her blond mane about. She had a trick of peering at men round it, like round the edge of a curtain. Very Veronica Lake. Poor Roy used to try and make her tie it back but she never did.'

'Roy?'

'The previous landlord, Roy Barton. Of course, Howard thought she was simply fantastic. Right up his street. He was always making lecherous remarks about her in Cornelia's hearing. He can be pretty crude, as I expect you know.'

'I've never actually met him.'

'Well, he's a bastard. But Crispin finds him good company and they've known each other ever since prep school, so I put up with him. I used to send them off to the pub together for a drink and Cornelia and I would stay behind.' She looked up at him. 'You think it could be Gunilla, don't you? So do I. It all adds up and, frankly, she was asking for trouble.'

'Did she have any particular admirers?'

'They *all* admired her – like I said – and she rang the changes. I suppose she'd get bored with them. When she arrived here, Ben Holland was the first in line.'

'Who is he?'

'Was. The grandson of old Mrs Holland who owned the farm that Howard bought. He was a good-looking kid, but not too bright. He used to follow Gunilla about like Mary's little lamb. Not long after, though, he got crushed to death when he overturned his tractor out in the fields. Except for his barmy grandmother, that was the end of the Holland family.'

Other guests came up and he talked to a brace of bankers and a QC and his wife before Cornelia reappeared.

'Do you mind if we leave, Hugh? I've got a dreadful headache.'

He drove her home in the Riley and, as they neared the house, she said, 'Where's Diego? He always opens the door.'

The front door remained stubbornly shut and it took a while for Cornelia to find a key in the depths of her handbag. Inside, everything was quiet and when she rang the servants' bell, nobody answered. She went off to the kitchen and came back, looking bewildered.

'They're not there, Hugh.'

'What about their room?'

The quarters occupied by the Filipino couple were bare. Clothes and possessions all gone. Not even a note left.

Cornelia wailed. 'I don't believe it . . . what rats! And they must have taken the Range Rover.' She collapsed on to a sofa. 'They might at least have done our lunch before they went.'

He went into the kitchen and found a frying pan and some eggs to make omelettes. He also found a packet of frozen peas in the freezer and cooked those too. They ate at the kitchen table, Cornelia picking fretfully at the peas.

'What on earth am I going to do, Hugh? I can't even boil an egg.'

'Ring up the agency. Get another couple.'

'You've no idea how hard it is to find decent people. They're like gold dust. And it's all because of that bloody skeleton. Diego and Perlita must have taken fright.'

'I imagine so.'

'Howard will be simply livid about the Range Rover.'

'I'll report it missing, Cornelia. I'm sure the police will find it.'

'Well, they can't seem to find anything else, can they? They're absolutely *useless*.'

He rang Naomi again.

'Do you think you could go on feeding Thursday for a bit longer? I'm still needed here.'

'*Prenez-garde*, Hugh!'

'I assure you there's no need to worry. How's Thursday?'

'He still looks at me daggers, but he's eating the food. And, before you ask, the garden's fine. I'm watering anything that needs it. It's a pity you're missing the irises – they're looking their best.'

'Yes, I'm sorry about that.'

He had planted them last year on Naomi's recommendation, in the mud at the edge of the pond – a yellow variety that apparently liked their feet in the water.

'And your Albertine is coming out.'

He wished he could see that too.

'Tell it to hang on until I get back.'

'It may not take any notice. By the way, your white lavender plants arrived yesterday, safe and sound. I'll look after them for you.'

'Thank you. I'd be very grateful.'

'I'll get Jacob to give the grass a cut. It could do with it.'

'That's a good idea. If he doesn't mind.'

'He'll need to get into your shed for the mower. Where do you keep the key to the padlock?'

He wouldn't put it past Naomi to have already been snooping in through the shed windows. He said reluctantly, 'It's on a hook by the back door.'

'I'll find it.'

He had no doubt that she would.

'How did the committee meeting go?'

'The usual wrangle. I made your apologies. Marjorie Cuthbertson was quite put out at your absence. Ruffled her feathers like a broody hen. They've got some pretty hare-brained schemes for this year. I'll tell you all about it when you get back . . . that's if you ever do.'

A loud guffaw. He held the receiver away from his ear.

'I'll be back as soon as I can, Naomi. And thanks.'

Eight

The Range Rover was discovered by the police, neatly parked at the main-line station, and the Colonel drove Cornelia over to collect it.

'I don't think there's any need to tell Howard about this, do you, Hugh?'

'None whatever.'

'He'd kick up the most tremendous fuss. Accuse them of stealing it. Get the police to prosecute.'

'Not much point in that.'

'I expect I'll find another married couple before he gets back.'

'I'm sure you will.'

'It's so lucky that you can cook, meantime.'

He smiled. 'I'm not sure I can.'

The immense freezer in the kitchen was full of food but the Colonel's off-by-heart repertoire was limited and there were no cookery books or any of Naomi's misspelled recipes to help him. He could manage a passable shepherd's pie, a roast chicken and some grilled pork, but it was a far cry from Perlita's delectable cuisine.

The agency who had originally supplied the Filipino couple had been unable to offer any alternatives and it took Cornelia several phone calls before she finally found one who had just taken a Swiss couple on to their books. She announced her intention of going to London to interview them.

'They sound quite possible, but, of course, I'll have to see them before I can make any decisions. Do you mind terribly keeping an eye on things here, Hugh?'

'Not at all.'

He took her to the station the next morning and when he returned the daily cleaning woman had arrived on her bike and was busy with the vacuum cleaner, steering it across the wood flooring. The Colonel went to sit out on the terrace with a book that he had found on the shelves – a leaden account of the Crimean War. Its chief merit was a fine old leather cover embossed with gold. The other books, he had noticed, had covers of similar quality which made him wonder whether they had all been bought by the yard for their looks, rather than their content. He couldn't imagine that Howard, and certainly not Cornelia, had the slightest interest in the long, drawn-out struggle with the Russians or in the gallant but useless charge of the Light Brigade, still less in Florence Nightingale's grim and grisly succour to the wounded and dying. In between pages, he observed the Heathcote's gardener at work. Old Matt, Cornelia had called him when she had warned that he would turn up to do what she described as potter about.

The Colonel watched the man working his way slowly and methodically through the borders – rooting out any hint of a weed, dead-heading, trimming and snipping. After a while, he put down his book and went over.

'Would you like a cup of tea?'

The gardener touched his cap. 'That's very kind

of you, sir. Milk and two sugars, if you please.'

He went away to search in the kitchen cupboards where he discovered a selection of exotic blends – orange blossom, cinnamon, peppermint, camomile and a box of Earl Grey. No sign of the ordinary cuppa kind that Old Matt would almost certainly prefer. He chose the Earl Grey as the least of the evils and carried the brew out in a bone-china cup and saucer, two sugars stirred in. When he complimented Old Matt on the gardens the old man shook his head.

'None of my doin', sir. They had one of those landscaper people in, and they always send someone to do the fancy clippin'. I just mow the lawn and keep things tidy.'

'Well, you do it very well.'

The gardener sucked at the tea. 'When Mrs Holland were alive she wouldn't have nothin' cut back. Roses ramblin' everywhere, shrubs overgrown. Bit of a mess, if the truth be told, but that were the way she liked it. To my mind, there's such a thing as bein' too tidy in a garden.'

Both men looked in silence at the faultless borders, the flawless lawn, the impeccable topiary. The Colonel wondered what Old Matt made of *Redemption.*

He said, 'You must have worked here for some years, then?'

'Close on forty. Mrs Holland's son, Mr Tim and his wife took over the farm till they got killed in a car crash and young Mr Ben inherited. He weren't interested in the garden – most farmers aren't – all they think of is crops and animals. Then Mr Ben went and got hisself killed on the

98

tractor and poor old Mrs Holland went inside the house and never came out no more, 'cept feet first. I would have retired then and there, but when the farm were sold to Mr and Mrs Heathcote they asked me to stay on. So I did, to oblige. I don't need to work, but it gives me somethin' to do.'

The Colonel said, 'Rather a shock about that skeleton turning up in the barn.'

'Nasty business. They think it might be that Swedish girl who worked in the pub, don't they? That's what I heard. Wouldn't surprise me. I used to see her sneakin' into the barn when she was meetin' Mr Ben. He was sweet on her and I s'pose they went up to the hayloft. There's still some old hay up there, you know. I can't say as I blame him – not with her looks. She was an eyeful, all right. But if someone did her in, it couldn't have been Mr Ben. She was still alive and kickin' after he was dead.'

'Did you ever see her go to the barn again, after Mr Ben's death?'

'Oh yes. She went there often. I'd see her walkin' through the orchard on her way, pinchin' apples and eatin' them. Once when I went into the barn, she threw an apple core down from the hayloft and hit me on the head. Leanin' over she was, with all that blond hair hangin', and she was laughin' away at me. I told her she was trespassin', but she just went on laughin'. Called herself Rapnuzzle, or somethin'.'

The Colonel smiled. 'Rapunzel. It's an old fairy tale about a beautiful girl imprisoned by a witch in a tower. When she lets her hair down out of the window a prince climbs up it to rescue her.'

Old Matt wagged his head. 'Well, I always thought there was somethin' daft about that girl.'

The Colonel carried the empty cup and saucer back into the house and washed them up. The Crimean War having palled, he took a walk down to the village to buy a newspaper. Vera was not behind the counter this time; Alice, the partner who did all the cooking, was in her place. He found the newspaper and took it over to pay.

'I'd like some of your wonderful-looking cakes, too, please. Which do you recommend?'

She blushed and some of the faded prettiness returned. 'Well, people seem to enjoy the éclairs very much but you might prefer the carrot cake, perhaps? Or the sticky ginger-and-pear?'

He smiled at her. 'It's not for me. I thought Mrs Heathcote needed cheering up. Do you happen to know which are her favourites?'

'The éclairs – especially the coffee ones.'

'In that case I'll take half a dozen, please.'

'I'll put them in a box for you. They'll keep in the fridge until she gets back.'

He realized that Alice, and presumably the whole village, knew that Cornelia had gone off to London. It was just the same in Frog End, of course. Nobody could go anywhere unobserved. Naomi always spoke of constant surveillance by the local KGB, which was probably no exaggeration.

He waited while the éclairs were placed carefully in a box which Alice began to tie with a length of silver ribbon. Fortnum & Mason could do no better.

He said casually, 'I've been hearing a lot about

a Swedish girl called Gunilla Bjork who worked at the Golden Pheasant four or five years ago. She seems to have made a big impression on everyone. Do you remember her?'

'Yes, I remember her.'

'It seems possible that the remains found in Mrs Heathcote's barn could be hers.'

'They couldn't be. She went back to Sweden.'

'So it was thought. But perhaps she didn't, after all?'

'I wouldn't know anything about that.'

'Did she ever come in here?'

'Sometimes.'

'I'm sure she loved your cakes. I don't suppose they have such things in Sweden.'

'I've no idea. I've never been there.'

He went on, wanting to keep Alice talking to see if he might learn something. 'People keep telling me how very striking she was.'

She had finished doing the bow and looked up at him. He caught a flash of some strong emotion in her eyes but it was gone before he could read it.

'She was nothing special.'

But Betty Turner had said she was beautiful, Susie Fellows had referred to her as a knockout and Old Matt had called her an eyeful.

He said, 'I hear that she had many male admirers in the village.'

'You shouldn't believe everything that people tell you.'

'No, of course not.' He agreed completely. In his experience, people seldom told the real truth and almost never the whole truth.

101

He paid for the éclairs and she handed the box over, looking at him without expression.

'There was nothing admirable about Gunilla Bjork, Colonel. She had no morals, no conscience, no scruples, no shame.'

Her voice had been perfectly quiet but the words were unequivocal. Clearly, Alice had done more than disapprove of the Swedish girl: she had hated her.

The Colonel was about to speak again, when Vera appeared from the back of the shop.

'I'll carry on now, Alice. You take a break.'

It was an order, rather than an offer and it was obeyed at once. He wondered how much of the conversation Vera had overheard.

She said, 'I'd appreciate it if you didn't talk to Alice about Gunilla Bjork, Colonel. It always upsets her.'

'I'm sorry. I didn't realize that.'

'You weren't to know. Is there anything else I can get for you?'

'No, thank you.'

He walked back along the high street, carrying the box of éclairs and his newspaper and well aware that he was being observed. The twitch of a curtain, a shadow behind a window pane, a glance over a shoulder, a head raised above a wall. As he neared Ester Simmons's cottage, he saw that she was out working in her front garden. When he stopped by her gate, she came over, hoe in hand. She was wearing the same shapeless tweed skirt and the same kind of plain blouse: her own particular uniform.

He raised his cap.

'A beautiful day, Miss Simmons.'

'We could do with some rain,' she said. 'The garden needs it.'

Gardeners, like farmers, were never satisfied.

'I'm sure Nature will oblige.'

She leaned on the hoe. 'The village gossip is that the Heathcotes' skeleton belonged to Gunilla Bjork.'

'No police identification has been made – so far as I am aware.'

'It adds up, though. The girl was Trouble with a capital T. Some are born that way.'

'What way, exactly?'

'Man mad.'

The expression was old-fashioned but to the point.

'She must have caused some problems in the village.'

'She did indeed.'

'Alice in the shop certainly wasn't complimentary about her.'

'She wouldn't have been.'

'Oh?'

'Vera very smitten, you see.'

'Ah.'

'Well, obviously, Vera's the 'man' of that partnership and the Swedish girl was up for anything. She didn't care who got hurt. It was all sport to her. Just a game. I see you've bought some of Alice's cakes.'

'Yes, they looked very good.'

'They are. I don't often go to the village shop myself. I go to the nearest supermarket once a month in my old car. It's not so pleasant but it's a lot cheaper.'

He said, 'I thought I'd take some éclairs to lift Mrs Heathcote's spirits.'

'I thought she was away.'

Obviously, the whole village *did* know that Cornelia had gone to London.

'Yes, but not for long.'

'First the skeleton turns up in her barn, then her servants walk out of her house. I'm not surprised that Mrs Heathcote's spirits need lifting. I gather you can cook, though, Colonel. That's fortunate.'

He wondered if Miss Simmons actually headed up the local KGB herself. If so, he really ought to congratulate her. She seemed to know everything.

'I'm not sure it could be described as cooking,' he said. 'I heat things on the stove and stir them around or put them in the oven for the time printed on the container. I can follow recipes if they're straightforward and don't involve anything too complicated.'

'That's about my level too, Colonel. If I read the words grind with a pestle and mortar, I turn the page.'

They talked gardening for a while. She was not as knowledgeable as Naomi, he realized, but she obviously had a similarly natural understanding of plants and planting and the indispensable green fingers to go with it. Some people could make any plant flourish, while others invariably caused them to wither and die. He supposed that he fell somewhere in between the two categories. There had been some gratifying successes, but there were still failures. For instance, he had yet to

104

grow a clematis successfully whereas Miss Simmons had one with mauve-blue blooms the size of saucers vigorously embracing an old tree stump. He'd never seen one like it.

'*Vyvyan Pennell*,' she said in answer to his question. 'My favourite. She starts early with double flowers and then produces single ones afterwards. Quite magnificent. And I like *Ernest Markham* and *Jackmanii*, too, but they don't put in an appearance until later in the season.'

'What's your secret, Miss Simmons?'

She said sharply, 'My secret? What secret? What do you mean?'

'How do you get a clematis to grow so well? I've never managed it.'

'I really don't know, Colonel.'

As he took his leave, she said, 'It can't be easy to make a positive identification from bones.'

'Forensic science seems to have made great strides. Apparently, these days they can tell a great deal from almost nothing.'

He raised his cap to her and she went back to her gardening.

At the Golden Pheasant, he stopped for a pint of the local beer. The young landlord, Kevin, was serving behind the bar.

'Would you care to see our lunch menu, sir? We can offer a range of snacks and sandwiches, or some more substantial home-cooked dishes, if you prefer.'

'That sounds like an excellent idea.'

He ordered the steak and kidney pie and settled himself at a table in the corner with his beer and newspaper. There were a dozen or so other people in the lounge bar but no inhabitant with briar pipe, walking stick and collie dog to be seen, nor any soft country burr to be heard. He listened, instead, to over-loud, clipped accents and to London talk: the latest must-see plays, the newest smart restaurants, the best holiday hideaways.

The barmaid, Betty Turner, came to his table with a placemat, cutlery and a linen napkin. She arranged them neatly before him.

'Still staying with Mrs Heathcote, sir?'

'For the time being.'

'I'm sure she's very glad to have your company just now, until this shocking business is cleared up. Have the police learned anything more, I wonder?'

She was doing rather more than wonder, he thought: her face was eager with curiosity.

'Not as far as I know.'

'Well, we'll hear as soon as there's some news, I dare say.'

She brought the steak and kidney pie, baked in its own earthenware dish, and a small bowl of vegetables.

'There you are, sir. I'm sure you'll enjoy it. The landlord's wife does the cooking herself.'

He enjoyed it very much and, when he went to pay at the bar, asked Kevin to pass on his compliments to his wife.

'I'll do that, sir. She'll be very pleased.'

'She must be a great help to you.'

'I couldn't manage without her. It's very hard to get a reliable cook, let alone one as good as Polly. I don't know how the Bartons coped, with Mrs Barton being unable to pull her weight. It

106

needs to be an equal partnership to stand a chance. Some people think running a pub's a nice, easy way to earn a living, but that's not true. It's very hard work indeed.'

'I'm sure. Did the Bartons serve food as well?'

'Not what I'd call proper food, sir. Nothing home-cooked. It all came frozen from a catering company and Mrs Barton heated it up in a microwave. She could manage that, with Betty giving her a hand. I'm not surprised they gave up in the end. They were getting on in years and when Mr Barton's health started to go downhill, it was curtains for them. No choice. I heard he died not long after they retired, but I think she's still alive.'

'Rather a sad story.'

'As I said, sir, it's a hard life.'

Nine

The Colonel walked on back to the house. From the gateway, he could see a black car parked by the front door alongside the Riley and, as he approached, Detective Chief Inspector Rodgers and his keen young sergeant emerged.

'I was hoping you'd turn up soon, sir.'

'Mrs Heathcote's away in London, Inspector.'

'Yes, we know that.'

Was there anybody who didn't know?

He said, 'What can I do for you?'

'I've got some information that you can pass on to Mrs Heathcote when she gets back.'

'You'd better come in to the house, then.'

Instead of negotiating the sofas, the Colonel went for the dining table chairs. Easier for all. They sat down.

'What did you want me to tell Mrs Heathcote?'

Beating about the bush was not the inspector's style.

'We've identified the skeleton as Gunilla Bjork.'

'I thought it might be.'

'She came from Uppsala, as Mrs Turner informed us. It wasn't too difficult to find out more about her through the Swedish police. They're very efficient.'

'I'm sure they are. What exactly did you find out?'

'She was born and brought up in comfortable

108

circumstances, but her father died when she was eleven years old. Her mother remarried and, according to her, Gunilla never got on with her stepfather from day one. There were endless rows over her behaviour as a teenager – wearing too much make-up, dressing tartily, staying out late, going with men. In the end, when she was eighteen, she walked out. Never said where she was going, or got in touch, just disappeared. They didn't report it to the police and it doesn't look like they made much of an effort to find her. The impression given was that they were glad to be rid of her. It didn't worry them that she had never even sent a postcard.'

He wasn't very surprised by the story. A girl like Gunilla was bound to have had a rocky background.

'How was the identification made?'

'Teeth. She'd gone to the same dentist in Uppsala since childhood and he'd kept all her records. She had very good teeth, with no cavities, but when she was twelve she fell off her bike and broke her two front teeth. The Swedish dentist confirmed that he'd capped them for her; dentists always know their own work. Identification was the easy part.'

'And the hard part?'

'Finding out who killed her, how, and why. The forensic people believe the blow to the skull was the cause of death but we don't know what instrument delivered it, except that, according to the experts, it wasn't made of metal.'

The Colonel thought of the flint stone he had picked up – the way it had fitted into his hand, its heavy weight, the lethal sharpness of its edge. The perfect tool for the job.

'A chunk of flint would make a pretty good weapon. And there's plenty of it lying around, including in the barn.'

'It's possible but it doesn't help us. The killer would have taken the stone away. Probably thrown it in the nearest pond or stream where it would be washed clean and look no different from the rest.'

'Man, or a woman?'

'Could have been either. Anger lends strength, Colonel. You'd be amazed how much. Given Gunilla Bjork's record of behaviour, it could have been either a very angry man, or an even angrier woman. The blow was administered to the back of the skull, from behind, so it would have been unexpected. No chance for her to defend herself, or put up a fight.'

'Do you know if she was killed in the barn? Or somewhere else?'

'It's impossible to say for certain. There are no tracks or traces after so long. My money's on the barn, though. No killer with any sense would want to risk being seen dragging a dead body around in the open. I think she was killed in there.'

The Colonel said, 'The Heathcotes' gardener used to work for the Holland family who owned the farm before them. As it happens, he remembers Gunilla Bjork rather well. He told me that the grandson, Ben Holland, was infatuated with her and she used to meet him in the barn. He thinks they went up to the hayloft. Apparently, there's still some hay there.'

'Yes, there is. Ideal for a roll. But the grandson was killed in a tractor accident before the Swedish girl went missing – which rules him out.'

'The gardener also said that she went there quite often on her own, *after* the grandson was killed. He'd see her walking through the orchard, eating apples and heading that way, and he knows she went up into the hayloft. Once, when he went into the barn she threw an apple core down and it hit him on the head. He said she was leaning over the edge of the hayloft with her blond hair hanging down, laughing at him. Apparently, she was playing at being Rapunzel – so she told him.'

'Rapunzel?'

'The girl in the fairy tale with the very long hair.'

'I can't say I've ever read any fairy tales, Colonel, though I've had plenty told to me. But from what we've learned about Gunilla Bjork from her mother, she was play-acting all the time. What is Mrs Heathcote's gardener's name?'

'She calls him Old Matt. I don't know his surname.'

'Make a note, Collins. We'll need to speak to him.'

The sergeant whipped out his biro and notebook and made the note.

The Colonel said, 'She could have gone on meeting other men there, don't you think, after the grandson had died? As you say, it was an ideal place.'

'I bet she did.'

'And she could have been killed up in the hayloft by one of them?'

111

'I don't think she was killed in the hayloft, Colonel. If she was, why not leave her up there, hidden under the hay? The barn wasn't being used any more. No need to go to all the trouble of hauling her down and burying her. I think someone was waiting for her when she paid it one of her little visits. Then whoever it was popped her under the earth out of sight.'

There was a pause. The sergeant was still busily making notes, whatever they were about.

The Colonel said, 'Has her suitcase been found?'

'Not much hope of that. It could have been dumped anywhere and rotted away by now. All we know is that when the landlord sacked her she left the Golden Pheasant and took all her belongings with her, including her case.'

'According to Mrs Turner.'

'As you say, Colonel, according to Mrs Turner. We've tracked down Mrs Barton, the landlord's wife, to an address in Poole and we'll be finding out what she can add to the picture.'

'So what next, Inspector?'

'We keep on looking for the murderer.'

'In the village?'

'Well, it's very possible that he, or she, lives in King's Mowbray. But the chance of establishing guilt and proving it, is remote.'

'Oh?'

'If a murder isn't solved within a few days of the crime, it may well never be solved. The trail grows cold very quickly, Colonel. And we're talking about four and a half years ago.' The chief inspector got to his feet. 'But we'll do our best.'

It would be a half-hearted investigation, the Colonel realized. Going through the motions. Another round of routine questioning, some more raking over the barn. By his own admission, after more than thirty years in the force, Detective Chief Inspector Rodgers no longer had the energy or patience for difficult cases. He liked the open-and-shut ones. Not riddles.

He said, 'How much longer before you retire, Inspector?'

'Eight months. I'm counting the days.'

The Colonel smiled. 'I wouldn't be in too much of a rush. In my experience, retirement can be rather a let-down.'

'Not in my case. I've got it all worked out.'

'What are you planning to do?'

'To grow irises, Colonel. Full time. I've been doing that for years in whatever spare time I have, which isn't much in this job.'

'Irises? That's interesting.'

'They're my only passion. My wife left me fifteen years ago and I haven't replaced her. Did you know they were named after Iris, the Greek goddess of the rainbow?'

'I'm afraid I didn't. They're beautiful flowers. I have some in my own garden.'

'Which kind?'

He said ruefully, 'I've forgotten the name. I planted them at the edge of my pond. My neighbour, who knows about these things, said they'd like the damp. They're in flower now.'

'Might be *pseudacorus* . . . tall, beardless, with branched stems and golden-yellow flowers?'

'That sounds about right.'

'There are hundreds of different kinds, you know. Different colours, different markings, different heights . . . all glorious. There isn't another flower to touch them, in my opinion. The Xiphium and dwarf Reticulata are the easiest to grow. Me, I go for Juno, Oncocyclus and Regelia. They're the hardest, but the most beautiful.'

It was an incongruous pairing – delicate, exquisite blooms with a burly, stubby-fingered policeman, but the inspector's zeal and the expertise were obvious. The Colonel could see Chief Inspector Rodgers winning prizes at the best horticultural shows, perhaps even at Chelsea? What he could not see was the murder of Gunilla Bjork ever being solved.

Cornelia came back from London two days later. The Colonel met her at the station, off the evening train. She was weighed down with expensive-looking carrier bags and he took them from her.

'I picked up a few things while I was there,' she said. 'And I popped into Fortnum's to stock up on some essentials.'

The essentials he saw at a glance were anything but essential: jars and pots and tins of the sort of gourmet delights that would probably lie unopened in the larder for months, or even years.

As they drove back, he told her about the police visit and the news that the skeleton belonged to Gunilla Bjork.

She said in a strained voice, 'Oh God . . . I suppose that means they'll be hanging around for ever, making a perfect nuisance of themselves.'

'Well, I'm afraid they'll be asking more questions, seeing if they can find any leads.'

'Leads? What leads could there possibly be? It happened years ago.'

'They have to do their job.'

'Wasting time over some foreign slut who deserved what she got?'

He said quietly, 'Murder is murder, Cornelia, whoever the victim.'

She shrugged. 'Sorry. Anyway, I telephoned Howard from London and he's still insisting that we sell the house at once. I'll have to ring up the agents and get someone round. I won't mention the skeleton.'

'I think you'll find they already know about it.'

'Well, they don't need to *say* anything, do they? Estate agents always leave out things they don't want buyers to know about.'

He smiled, remembering the blurb on Pond Cottage – the liberal use of the word 'potential' and the failure to mention small drawbacks like death-watch beetle, rising damp, a falling roof, dangerous wiring, barely-existent plumbing and decay throughout. It would be child's play to a good estate agent to get round the problem. They might even use it as a feature? *Historic barn incorporating fascinating relic from the past.*

He said, 'Did you have any luck with the Swiss couple?'

'They seemed all right. Rather dull, but then the Swiss always are, aren't they?'

Cornelia obviously kept her nationalities in watertight compartments. The Swedish were all blond and blue-eyed, the Swiss all dull. Doubtless

115

her Italians were all excitable ice-cream sellers, her Scots all red-headed skinflints, her French all romantic lovers, and her Irish all drunks.

'How soon could they start?'

'The week after next. We'll have to cope somehow until then, Hugh. You don't mind, do you?'

In the kitchen, he took the Fortnum's essentials out of their classy carrier bag. Stuffed pimentos, chargrilled aubergines, wild asparagus tips, roasted artichoke hearts, sun-kissed tomatoes, baby squid, kalamata olives, king crabs' legs, dried porcini mushrooms, terrine of venison, a large tin of foie gras and a pot of Gentlemen's Relish. He put them away in the cupboard. For supper, he fried some outsize scallops that he had hunted down in the freezer and boiled the new potatoes that Old Matt had dug up in the vegetable garden. A fresh young lettuce, also grown by the gardener, provided a salad; all he had to do was make the dressing, which he'd memorized from Naomi. For pudding, he produced the éclairs. Cornelia was delighted.

'What a treat! I simply love them. How did you know I liked the coffee ones.'

'Alice told me. She happened to be serving at the counter and I had a bit of a chat with her.'

'Oh? She's not usually very forthcoming. Tends to stay out of sight, behind the scenes.'

'We talked about Gunilla Bjork, as a matter of fact.'

'Not that wretched girl, again! Sorry, Hugh, but do you mind not mentioning her. I'm so sick of the subject.'

'I'm sure you must be. But I was curious to know what Alice thought of her. She was actually very forthcoming. She told me that for all the male admirers, there was nothing admirable about the Swedish girl. That she had no morals, no conscience, no scruples and no shame.' He smiled drily. 'Clearly, she'd loathed her and I wondered if there was a particular reason. Ester Simmons enlightened me later on, when I was passing by her cottage. Apparently, Vera was very smitten by Gunilla. Alice was jealous.'

'Gracious, you *have* been busy, Hugh!'

'As I said, I was curious.'

'Well, I can't tell you anything more, if that's what you're hoping. As far as I know, Vera and Alice have always been devoted to each other. They're like an old married couple.'

'Even old married couples sometimes stray.'

Cornelia jabbed at an éclair and cream spurted on to her plate.

'That's true.'

He wondered how often Howard strayed, given the unlimited opportunities on his travels; and whether he had ever visited Gunilla's hayloft; and whether Cornelia had found out?

Ten

A representative from the estate agents summoned by Cornelia arrived on the doorstep the following day. The Colonel, in his butler's capacity, opened the door to him. A card was proffered.

'Good morning to you, sir. Henry Willoughby from Parnall, Monk and Morrison. Mrs Heathcote is expecting me.'

They had clearly sent one of their senior men. There was none of the callow brashness of the young lad who had shown the Colonel round Pond Cottage. No creased blazer or scuffed suede shoes; instead, well-cut tweeds, well-polished brogues and well-oiled discretion.

Cornelia received him graciously and the Colonel retreated to soldier on with the Crimean War, while she took the estate agent on a lengthy tour of the house. As they progressed, he could hear Hans Birger's name being mentioned several times by Cornelia, and Mr Willoughby's duly-impressed responses.

After a while, the Crimean War began to pall once again and the Colonel picked up a weekly local newspaper which had been delivered. The Danish architect would certainly have categorized it as clutter. On the front page was a report on the identification of the mysterious skeleton in the barn, together with a photograph of Gunilla Bjork, presumably obtained by the

118

Swedish police. She was wearing an off-the-shoulder white peasant blouse – the sort that Jane Russell wore in *The Paleface* – and she was peering round a curtain of long blond hair, just as Susie Fellows had described. And, as Betty Turner had accurately said, she was beautiful. Exceptionally so. He could see what all the fuss had been about. It was impossible to believe that such youth and beauty could have turned into the grinning skull and dry bones that he had seen in the barn.

Cornelia and the estate agent returned from the tour.

'Hugh, would you be a dear and show Mr Willoughby the gardens and everything?' Cornelia paused. 'And the barn, too. I'm afraid I'm really not up to it.'

He led the way out on to the terrace, and the estate agent followed, murmuring aside into a small tape recorder as they went along. His comments were entirely predictable: *immaculately landscaped gardens . . . mature topiary . . . luxurious mosaic-tiled, illuminated swimming pool, complete with spring-board and large jacuzzi . . . changing cabins with showers as well as a spacious refrigerator with ice-maker . . . built-in barbecue with a delightful canopied area for entertaining guests. All-weather tennis court in perfect condition and charming pavilion, also with refrigerator and verandah for spectators. Magnificent medieval barn, recently fully restored . . .*

They went into the barn, ducking under blue and white police tape without comment. Mr Willoughby admired the interior, craning his neck

119

upwards. *Re-roofed with authentic old tiles, retaining almost all the original roof timbers, and featuring an interesting old hayloft with access by ladder* . . .

It was a considerable height, the Colonel thought, gazing upwards too. He could quite see why Gunilla Bjork, with her long blond tresses, had played at being Rapunzel imprisoned in the tower. A fantasy that had somehow gone hideously wrong.

The estate agent indicated the cordoned-off area.

'I take it that's where the unfortunate discovery was made?'

There wasn't much point denying it. 'Yes, indeed. In the corner.'

'Mrs Heathcote didn't mention it to me but, of course, I'm well aware of the situation. It's been reported in the national and local press. I must admit it presents some problems at the moment, but nothing that need worry us in the longer term.'

The Colonel said drily, 'You mean that a corpse won't put buyers off?'

Mr Willoughby shook his head. 'Not at all. This is a very desirable property, in perfect order, with superb amenities and in an excellent and exclusive location. It ticks all the boxes, as they say. We simply wait while the police conclude their investigations, and in the meantime we plan our marketing strategy.'

They walked over to the corner and stared down at the shallow grave.

The estate agent said, 'I gather from the newspapers that it was some Swedish girl who worked in the Golden Pheasant pub. From her photo, she rather looked as though she asked for it.'

'People don't usually ask to die.'

'You know what I mean. Well, let's hope the police get a move on and find the culprit soon. The trouble is, with a girl like that it could be anybody.'

Mr Willoughby switched on the tape recorder again.

The barn would make a superb games room and allows ample space for both table tennis and billiards. Alternatively, it could be used as a gymnasium and could accommodate a wide variety of exercise machines and aids, even, possibly, an indoor swimming pool . . .

Cornelia reappeared as they returned to the house and the Colonel left her on the terrace for a final discussion with the estate agent.

He went back to his chair and picked up the local newspaper again, studying the photograph of Gunilla Bjork once more. Mr Willoughby had thought that she rather looked as though she'd asked for it, which was unfair, as well as inaccurate. Women were entitled to wear their hair how they liked and dress how they liked without anybody having the right to murder them. But the estate agent had been right that anybody could have done so. The most obvious motives were jealousy, hatred, frustration, revenge – or simply in order to stop her from spilling the beans?

The telephone rang and he answered it. Crispin Fellows was at the other end of the line, inviting him for bridge that evening after dinner.

'One of our regular four has gone sick on us,

Colonel. Can you step into the breach? It's all men and decent stakes. No bloody women around. Susie always takes herself off to bed early.'

Bridge was something he'd always enjoyed. 'I'd be glad to.'

'Nine o'clock, then?'

'I'll be there.'

Earlier, he had fished in the freezer and brought out tuna steaks to grill for supper. Cornelia's Fortnum & Mason jar of grilled aubergines was liberated from the kitchen cupboard to be heated up and the rest of Old Matt's potatoes put in a pot and boiled. It was an unusual combination but perfectly edible.

Afterwards, Cornelia went off to watch television while the Colonel drove over to the Fellows' house. The other two players had already arrived – Brigadier Lawrence whom he remembered from the Sunday drinks and an Edward Maplin who was introduced as the owner of the local brewery responsible for the excellent ale served in the Golden Pheasant.

Crispin Fellows was partnering the brewer and the Colonel sat down opposite the Brigadier.

'What are we playing for?'

'A pound a point, Colonel,' Fellows said. 'All right by you?'

In Frog End it was usually a penny a point but this was King's Mowbray.

'That's fine. What convention do you play, Brigadier?'

'Simple Acol.'

They played the best of three rubbers and the Colonel and the Brigadier were lucky in the third rubber. The losers paid up and there was only a brief post-mortem – also unlike in Frog End where Major Cuthbertson was likely to replay almost every hand.

'We would have made it but the kings were on the wrong side,' Edward Maplin said, but without resentment.

The Brigadier grunted. 'And you missed trumping that Jack of Clubs.'

They moved away from the bridge table to sit in comfortable armchairs, and brandy and cigars were produced. The Colonel was reminded of many evenings spent in messes and clubs during his army career, at home and abroad. He enjoyed the company of women very much but sometimes it was a relief to be without them. Restrictions were lifted, speech franker, opinions more honest. The Brigadier's were franker than most.

'Damned politicians! They're nothing but a pack of scoundrels. Not an honest man among them. No principles, no guts. Kowtowing to the bloody Europeans, opening the floodgates for all kinds of foreign riff-raff to come and claim every benefit they can get their dirty hands on.'

'Tut-tut, Jumbo,' Crispin Fellows said. 'You mustn't talk like that any more. It's forbidden. You'll be taken away and clapped in irons for being racist.'

'I *am* racist and proud of it. The British are the finest people on earth – except for our politicians – and I'm not afraid to say so loud and clear. Unlike your snivelling Lefties.'

'They're not mine, Jumbo.'

123

'Didn't mean it literally. We used to be proud to be British – not that we've ever blown our trumpets about it. Not our style. But look at what we've been reduced to! Our armed forces cut to a handful of men, half a dozen ships and a few obsolete planes. Beholden to the bloody Yanks. Even the French can put on a better show, for God's sake. We're the laughing stock of the world. Isn't that so, Colonel?'

He said mildly, 'We're certainly no longer the power we used to be but I believe we're still well respected.'

'Huh! What do you think, Maplin?'

'I agree with the Colonel. There's still plenty for us to be proud of. Lots to recommend us. That's why so many foreigners want to come and live here.'

Crispin Fellows groaned. 'Don't start him off on that again, for God's sake.'

The conversation took a different turn – in the direction of fishing – which provoked another outburst from the Brigadier who had been having no luck on his stretch of the river and blamed it all on pollution.

'Nothing to do with your brewery, Maplin, of course. It's those holiday campers and their bloody caravans, dumping all kinds of rubbish, using it as a sewer. And some fool on a TV nature programme went and let a pair of otters go free. It took us years to get rid of the damned things and now we've got them back again. We won't have a single fish left soon.'

The talk eventually came round to the subject of Gunilla Bjork and the police investigation into

124

her death. It was Crispin Fellows who had brought it up.

'You remember her, don't you, Jumbo? The Swedish bombshell at the pub?'

'Vaguely.'

'A bit more than vaguely, old chap. Let's face it, we all remember her vividly. Isn't that so, Edward?'

'I wouldn't put it quite as strongly as that.'

'Well, we're all suspects in the eyes of the police – every man and woman who was living in or around King's Mowbray five years ago. Any one of us might have done it.'

'Steady on! That's going a bit far.'

'Is it? I wouldn't say so, Edward. Would you, Jumbo?'

'Bloody ridiculous, is what I say. Damned police don't know their job. Haven't a clue.'

'They've probably got several clues, if we did but know it. When you think about it, we were all involved with Gunilla, one way and another.'

'Speak for yourself, Fellows.'

'Actually, she didn't really appeal to me – rather over the top, I always thought – but I don't think you were exactly immune, Jumbo, if I remember rightly. Or you, Edward. But you were hardly the only ones. She played the same game with pretty well every male, and that included poor old Vera. Isn't that the truth?'

The Brigadier growled. 'I wouldn't know. All I know is I wish to God she hadn't been dug up. Gives the village a bad name. Next thing we know property prices will start falling.'

'And we certainly wouldn't want that to happen. So, the sooner the crime is solved, the better.'

The Brigadier drained his brandy and consulted his watch. His face was flushed. 'Time I made a move. No idea it was so late.'

The brewer stood up as well. 'I ought to be off too. Early meeting tomorrow.'

Crispin Fellows showed the two men to the door and returned.

'You'll stay for another brandy, Colonel?'

He accepted, but not for the sake of the drink. People's reactions to any mention of Gunilla Bjork were interesting to him.

Crispin Fellows refilled their glasses.

'Poor old Jumbo, tilting away at windmills, as ever. Phyllis will probably be waiting behind the door with a rolling pin. You've met his wife, haven't you?'

'Seen, not actually met.'

'One glance tells all. Not exactly Cleopatra, is she? And they've been married for ever. It's a sad fact for us men that by the time we wake up to the fact that life's passing us by, it's too late to do anything about it. Jumbo thought he'd got it made with Gunilla but it was a joke, of course. She was just teasing him, leading him up the garden path. Very cruel of her. Gave him her come-hither look from behind the blond curtain and made him feel young and virile again. Edward's wife's a lot easier on the eye than Phyllis but he was very taken by Gunilla, too. As I said, I might have been tempted myself, but she wasn't really my type and also I'm very satisfied with my third wife. Besides, I haven't a head for heights.'

'Heights?'

'It was always the hayloft. God knows why. Gunilla had some sort of weird thing about the place. She wanted men climbing that bloody great ladder for her while she waited at the top dangling her long blond hair.'

'Rapunzel,' the Colonel said.

'What?'

'The beautiful girl in the old fairy tale. That's who Gunilla was pretending to be. A witch imprisoned her at the top of a tall tower and a prince had to climb up a plait of her long golden hair to rescue her. *Rapunzel, Rapunzel, let down your hair.* Don't you remember?'

'Christ! I can't say I do. The Three Billy Goats Gruff was more my mark. *Trip-trap, trip-trap. Who's that trip-trapping over my bridge?* Did the prince make it?'

'Yes he did, but the witch found out and tricked him that Rapunzel was dead. He threw himself from the tower into some thorn bushes and was blinded.'

'Poor guy.'

'Fortunately, everything works out in the end and he and Rapunzel lived happily ever after.'

'It's not often like that in real life, is it? Unless you're very lucky.'

'Unfortunately not.' The Colonel drank some more brandy. 'How did you know about the hayloft and the ladder?'

'Gossip. Half the village probably knew, though they'll never admit it. The police are wasting their time trying to nail down the culprit. No one's going to help them, and, as I said, it could be anybody.'

127

'But some might have had more of a motive than others?'

'Well, it's possible that Jumbo might have decked her in a rage. She spread it around that he couldn't make it up the ladder, or anything else, which was probably quite true. I can imagine him puffing and panting up the rungs with his tongue hanging out, can't you? Gunilla made him look a complete ass. And he's not the sort of chap to forgive that.'

'Who else had a motive?'

'Well, let me see. I'm pretty sure Edward fancied his chances in the hayloft, but I don't know if he ever actually got up there. Maybe he did and Gunilla threatened to tell his wife, Sonia. Or maybe she found out, anyway, and got in a jealous rage. You don't tangle with Sonia, if you can help it. Or Alice might have done the deed because Vera fancied Gunilla, or perhaps Gunilla led Vera up the garden path like Jumbo and then dumped her. The possibilities and permutations are endless. Even our worthy rector might have entertained sinful and lustful thoughts beneath his surplice – though that one's pretty unlikely, I must admit. As a matter of fact, Cornelia had a *double* motive.'

'How do you mean?'

'Well, Howard's the obvious motive, of course. He certainly had the hots for Gunilla – nothing unusual in that. But Gunilla tried it on with Cornelia's precious Rory when they were staying with us. He was only a kid and I don't think anything much happened, but there was an almighty row. Howard went berserk and Cornelia

128

was frantic. She felt her son had been besmirched for ever. I bet he enjoyed it, though.' Crispin Fellows puffed at his cigar. 'I'm sure I could scare up some more suspects, if you like.'

'How about Miss Simmons?'

'Dame Slap? Can't quite see a motive there, unless she simply thought Gunilla needed eliminating like one of her garden weeds. Or maybe she had a guilty secret from her past that Gunilla had somehow found out about? Abusing a pupil, say . . . that makes for a very juicy scandal these days. The newspapers love that sort of thing and so do their readers. Gunilla was always pretending and teasing, like I told you. Playing cat and mouse with people. To be perfectly honest, she bloody well asked for what she got.'

The estate agent, Mr Willoughby, had voiced the same view. So had Cornelia, come to that, and so had Susie Fellows. The Colonel guessed that most people would think it, though they might not actually say so.

He said, 'I gather that the former landlord of the Golden Pheasant eventually gave her the sack.'

'Roy was a cretin to have hired her in the first place. She brought the customers in all right but she never did a stroke of work.'

'So, nobody was very surprised when she disappeared from the village?'

'No. We all assumed she'd gone off to the bright lights of London, or back to Sweden.'

'Except one person.'

'Well, yes . . . The one who did her in. Why the interest, anyway, Colonel?'

'I'm just curious.'

'Be careful. Curiosity killed the cat.'

Driving back, he thought about a particular cat – the battle-scarred, black and tan old stray who had condescended to move into Pond Cottage and live with him. It wouldn't do to leave Thursday on his own much longer or he might decide to cancel their arrangement and move out, which would be a great pity. The Colonel had grown accustomed to having him around. As soon as the Swiss couple arrived, he'd leave Cornelia in their, no doubt, very capable hands and head for home.

Later, in bed and waiting for sleep, he thought again about Gunilla Bjork. Whatever her character and shortcomings, she had not deserved to die: to have her young life brutally cut short. Crispin Fellows had been right that almost anyone in King's Mowbray might have done it and Detective Chief Inspector Rodgers was going to find it very difficult to track down the culprit. The trail was too old and too cold, as he'd said himself. Added to that, the inspector's heart would not be in the search: he was too much in love with Iris, the goddess of the rainbow.

The Colonel went through some suspects in his mind: Alice at the shop, Vera herself, the Brigadier humiliated by his failure, his stoutly-built wife, Phyllis, who looked more than capable of wielding any weapon, the brewer, Edward Maplin, or his wife, Sonia, who was not to be tangled with. Howard Heathcote, Cornelia, a thirteen-year-old Rory . . . and heaven knew how many others in the village. Crispin Fellows could well have lied about Gunilla not being his type which meant that Susie Fellows would also have had a good reason to be jealous. Ester Simmons would have been on his list of non-runners, together with the rector and Old Matt, but the offhand suggestion of some guilty secret in her past had made him think again. Pupil abuse in a sexual form seemed a ludicrous idea, but perhaps she had administered the cane unnecessarily hard and gone beyond the acceptable boundaries of discipline, even for those Dame Slap schooldays? *My secret? What do you mean?* She had snapped out the words at him. He had meant her secret for growing clematis, but she had reacted oddly. The modern trend was for grown-up people to reveal any childhood abuse – real or imagined – and their stories were gleefully reported in the newspapers. No, Ester Simmons could not be ruled out, after all.

There was no shortage of potential murderers, the Colonel thought to himself. Only a shortage of evidence.

Eleven

'Rory phoned me from Harrow while you were out playing bridge,' Cornelia said at breakfast. 'He's got an exeat this weekend and he's coming home tomorrow for a night.'

'You don't look very happy about it.'

She was fiddling with her coffee cup, twisting the handle to and fro.

'I'm worried, Hugh. Someone told him about the skeleton – they'd read about it in the papers – and he seems to think it's a big joke. He wants to see what he calls the "scene of the crime".'

'Boys can be very gruesome.'

'It will be lovely to have him, of course, but, to be honest, I'd much sooner he didn't come here at the moment. I don't want him mixed up in this sordid business.'

'There's no reason why he should be – is there?'

'No . . . It's nothing whatever to do with him. The whole thing's just so unpleasant.' More twisting the cup handle. 'I wish to heavens the police would go away and leave us in peace. That awful tape is still up. I can't think why.'

'I'll phone the Chief Inspector and ask if he can do something about it, if you like.'

'Thank you, Hugh. You're such a comfort.'

'More coffee?'

'Just a drop.'

When he had poured the coffee, he said, 'Rory

was thirteen when Gunilla Bjork was working at the Golden Pheasant. That's a very impressionable age. I wonder if she tried to impress him – when you were staying with the Fellows?'

'What on *earth* do you mean?'

'Targeting a good-looking thirteen-year-old boy would have been an amusing diversion – a change from all the older men slavering after her. That's what I mean, Cornelia.'

She covered her eyes with her hand and he waited until she took it away.

'If you must know, Hugh, that bitch did try to get her claws into Rory. Luckily, we found out and stopped it at once. I could have killed her for contaminating my son . . . I don't mean that literally, of course.'

'How did you find out?'

'Howard caught her with him in the garden at the back of the Golden Pheasant. There's a brook there and Howard and Crispin took Rory with them one evening so he could fish while they were drinking in the pub. When Howard went to fetch him, he found Gunilla lying with him on the bank and she was kissing him. Thank God, it wasn't worse! Howard was absolutely *livid*. I've never seen him so angry. He told Gunilla if she ever laid a finger on Rory again, he'd make sure that she was thrown out of the country.'

'So Rory never went to the barn to meet her?'

'He didn't know anything about the barn, Hugh. How on earth could he? He was only in King's Mowbray once or twice when we stayed with Susie and Crispin.'

'You don't think Gunilla might have suggested

it to him when they were lying on the bank together?'

'Even if she did, Rory would never have had the opportunity. After that episode, he was with us all the time. We made sure of that.'

He said slowly, 'Did *you* know about the barn, Cornelia? Did you know that Gunilla was in the habit of daring her lovers to climb the ladder into the hayloft in order to claim her? That she pretended to be Rapunzel in the fairy tale? Letting her hair hang over the side?'

'I most certainly did *not*. What a tramp she was! And she must have been mad, too.' She shivered and rubbed her arms. 'This house gives me the absolute creeps now. I can't think how I ever liked it. Howard's right, the sooner we get rid of it, the better.'

Rory turned up the following afternoon. He had been given a lift from Harrow by the family of one of his school friends. The Colonel observed his arrival with interest – Cornelia fawning on her son, his impatient response, his studiedly casual wave of thanks to the friend and family as they drove off in their green Bentley. The Colonel realized that the tall and good-looking Rory was, unfortunately, his father's son.

He was deputed by Cornelia to give a guided tour of the scene of the crime.

'You don't mind, do you, Hugh? I really couldn't bear to go anywhere near the place.'

'Not at all.'

He conducted the young man over to the barn, police tape still gratifyingly in place, and showed him the shallow grave where Gunilla Bjork's body had lain undisturbed for nearly five years.

'Wow! Awesome!'

He had found it quite awesome himself.

'It's upset your mother a lot. I shouldn't talk about it too much, if I were you.'

'I don't know why she'd care. She hated Gunilla.'

'Did she really?'

'Loathed her. I think Dad rather fancied her, that's why.'

'Do you remember Gunilla yourself?'

'Oh, absolutely! She was working at the pub when we stayed in King's Mowbray with the Fellows.'

'What did you think of her?'

The young man ran a hand through his forelock. 'Well, she was frightfully attractive . . . lots of long blond hair and fantastic boobs. I remember her jumping me once. She came up behind me on the bank where I was fishing at the back of the pub and the next thing I knew her tongue was down my throat and her hand down my jeans. I was only about thirteen and Dad came out and found us. He kicked up a hell of a stink. So did Ma. But I thought it was fantastic, I can tell you. First time anything like that had happened to me.'

'Did Gunilla ever ask you to meet her here, in the barn?'

'No, worse luck. I'd have gone like a shot, if she had. We were only there for the weekend and I went straight back to Harrow.'

'You didn't meet her again?'

Rory shook his head. 'She wasn't working at

the pub any more the next time we stayed with the Fellows. She'd left the village – or at least everybody thought she had.' He stared, fascinated, at the hollow in the earth. 'I say, you saw her, didn't you? When they'd found her. What did she look like?'

'Just dry bones,' he said. 'That's all.'

'Awesome!'

The visit to the barn was clearly the high spot of the weekend for Rory. The Colonel watched and listened with sympathy to Cornelia's attempts to entertain and amuse her son while he went on looking bored. He volunteered to play a few sets of tennis with the young man, being careful to lose. Winning, he knew, would not have been a good idea.

Over dinner at the Golden Pheasant, Cornelia brought up the subject of the eighteenth birthday dance.

'I've got everything planned,' she told her son. 'The caterers, the flowers, the jazz band . . . everything. With luck, the police will have finished soon, won't they, Hugh? Then the builders will be back to do the barn floor and it will all be ready in time. I thought a steel band might be rather fun to have as well.'

'Steel bands are history, Ma.'

'Oh. I didn't realize that.'

Rory said, 'Actually, I was thinking that it might be rather cool to do something in London instead. Go down the Thames on a boat, maybe, or take over the Zoo. Make it a bit different, you know.'

* * *

On Sunday, the Colonel drove Cornelia's son to the station to catch the train back to London. They bowled merrily along the lanes.

'Dad's going to buy me a Porsche for my eighteenth.'

'Is he really? That's a wonderful present.'

'Yeah . . .'

The Colonel smiled to himself. He could tell that Rory wasn't at all sure what to make of the old Riley – whether it was awesomely cool or simply pathetic.

Detective Chief Inspector Rodgers was at his desk when the Colonel telephoned on Monday morning about the scene-of-the-crime tape. He sounded in an affable mood.

'I'll send someone to remove it. Not much point in leaving it there any longer. We've gone over the place with a fine toothcomb.'

'No further news on the case?'

'Nothing to speak of. The landlord's wife, Mrs Barton, is in hospital, in Poole General. Apparently, she's been stuck in there for months. I sent Sergeant Collins off to have a chat with her, but it was a waste of time. Her kidneys have packed up completely and she's too ill to answer questions. Collins said she wouldn't even open her eyes.'

It reminded the Colonel of Naomi's visit to his own sick bed, armed with the chicken soup, and of himself taking refuge in the same way.

'That's unfortunate. She might have been able to shed some useful light on the case.'

'I doubt it. As I said before, most people can't remember what happened last week.'

'But she would have known Gunilla Bjork rather well. Seen her in action, as it were.'

'So would most of the village. I've already got a bloody good idea of what made that girl tick and I don't think a sick old lady would be able to add much to the general picture.'

'Perhaps her husband could have done?'

'Well, we'll never know that, will we? Dead men can't talk.'

That was indisputable.

'Will you keep Mrs Heathcote posted?'

'If there's anything to post.'

'You're not optimistic?'

'No, Colonel, I'm not. I'm realistic. The reality is that we're not very likely to solve this particular case. The file will probably end up gathering dust on a shelf with all the rest.'

After he had replaced the receiver, the Colonel strolled over to the barn, ducked under the police tape and went inside. He had no idea what he was searching for. There were certainly no clues to be seen. The barn was bare, except for the old wooden ladder reaching up to the hayloft. He gripped its sides with both hands and looked up the rungs. Thirty feet at least, he reckoned, and at a near vertical angle. No wonder the Brigadier had failed the test. It was tough enough to test the nerve of all but the young and fit. A classic challenge for an aspiring and hot-blooded lover, with the reward beckoning tantalizingly at the top.

He thought again of the story of Rapunzel and her valiant prince climbing up the plait of golden hair to the top of the tall tower and of his fall into the thornbushes to be blinded. Gunilla's suitors had been luckier. They had survived their trial unscathed. But supposing there had been a twist to the modern version of the fairy tale? Supposing Gunilla herself had fallen? Or been pushed? He picked up a large chunk of flint stone from the barn floor, tested its weight and felt its sharpness.

Twelve

As usual, the Colonel walked down to the village for his newspaper, encountering a woman walking her black Labrador dog. He recognized her as the one who had given him directions when he had first driven into King's Mowbray. She also recognized him and stopped to talk.

'I'm Sonia Maplin,' she said. 'I believe you played bridge with my husband.'

She was certainly easier on the eye than the Brigadier's wife, and a good deal younger. Not a paid-up member of the coven, he decided.

Her style was different.

'Yes, indeed.'

'I hear you're rather good, Colonel.'

He smiled. 'I've put in plenty of practice over the years.'

'It's a very good game, isn't it? I play once a week with a regular women's four and whenever else I get the chance. I never get bored of it, do you?'

'Not so far.'

'Every hand's different – that's the joy. Always a challenge, don't you find?'

'Very much so.'

'Rory was home over the weekend, wasn't he?'

How on earth had she known? Simple, though, when he thought about it: she was always out walking the dog. A one-woman reconnaissance patrol.

'Yes, that's right.'

'How is he?'

'He seemed to be very well.'

'Growing up fast, I imagine. Not too much like his father, I hope. And Cornelia?'

'She's well, too.'

'I'd call, but we've never been close. Edward and I objected to the original farmhouse being knocked down and to that hideous place they had built instead. It should never have been allowed, but there you are. My husband's family have lived in King's Mowbray for a hundred and fifty years, and everything's changed in the last twenty.'

'It happens everywhere, I'm afraid.'

'Rather ironical that the Swedish girl should have been found in the Heathcotes' barn.'

'Ironical?'

'A sort of comeuppance, I thought, for the way they steamrollered the old farmhouse. And I wasn't sorry to hear that that girl had got her just desserts either. She richly deserved it.'

It was amazing how openly vindictive perfectly pleasant-seeming people could be. He'd noticed it many times.

'She seems to have upset a lot of people.'

'She did, Colonel. But we won't go in to all that. Let's just say, nobody's shedding any tears for Gunilla Bjork.'

The Labrador, who had been waiting patiently, started to tug at his lead and, with a wave of her hand, Sonia Maplin strode on down the lane.

* * *

141

The coven was assembled in the village shop – the same four women, picking over the latest rumours, ash-blond heads together.

'I'm not a bit surprised it turned out to be that Swedish girl,' one said. 'She was bound to come to a bad end, sooner or later.'

There was unanimous agreement.

'All that awful dyed hair,' another said. 'It was a joke!'

'Actually, to be fair, Lois, I think it was real. A lot of Swedes have hair that colour and men always seem to fall for it. Hook, line and sinker. Remember the Brigadier making a complete fool of himself?'

'He wasn't the only one, was he?'

The Colonel took his time, browsing along the shelves. More names were mentioned – some he knew, most he didn't. Agreement was reached over the incompetence of the police, the unlikelihood of the crime ever being solved and the fact that it didn't much matter anyway. Gunilla Bjork had only got what she deserved. The shop bell jangled loudly as the coven dispersed.

The Colonel emerged with his newspaper. Vera was standing behind the counter, impassive as always. He would have been interested to know her thoughts.

As he paid, he said pleasantly, 'Beautiful day, isn't it?'

'Very nice.'

'I don't suppose you get much time for sitting in the sun.'

'I don't get much time to sit anywhere. Nor does Alice.'

'No, I shouldn't think she does.'

'As a matter of fact, we're thinking of selling up.'

'Really? That would be a sad loss to the village.'

'We're not very concerned about the village,' she said. 'It's not the place it was when we first arrived here. We've come to that conclusion.'

He took the change she was holding out. 'Do you have somewhere else in mind?'

'Norfolk. I used to go there for holidays as a child, and Alice likes the idea of living by the sea. There's something clean and honest about it.'

'I know what you mean. Would you open another shop?'

'I don't think so. The business would be too seasonal, and it's time we retired. Alice hasn't been well recently.'

'I'm sorry to hear that.'

'The business over Gunilla Bjork has upset her a lot.'

'Yes, she seemed rather distressed about it.'

'She hated Gunilla, you know.'

'But you didn't?'

'I fell under her spell, Colonel, if you want the truth, and she treated me like she treated all the rest. She was completely heartless. In the end, I hated her as much as Alice did. We neither of us had anything to do with her death, but it was a very painful episode for us, and still is. So, it's better we move away from here, you see. Close the door behind us.'

'Well, I'm sure you'll both be missed.'

'Oh, I don't think so. We'll sell to someone

who'll keep up the same standard. That's all these people will care about.'

He was not very surprised by her assessment of the residents of King's Mowbray.

'I'll be leaving myself, as a matter of fact. Mrs Heathcote has a replacement couple arriving next week and her husband will be returning soon from abroad.'

'I hear the property is on the market. I wonder if they'll find a buyer, considering what happened there.'

'Oh, I shouldn't think there'll be too much difficulty. The estate agents don't seem to think it will make any difference.'

She looked at him steadily. 'Life moves on, doesn't it, Colonel? Gunilla Bjork will soon be forgotten.'

'Yes,' he said. 'I expect she will.'

'You won't mention what I just told you – about us leaving?'

'Of course not.'

'I know I can trust you.'

How does she know, he wondered, as he walked back through the village. How can she be so certain? Why did people place such blind faith in him? Extraordinary.

He should, he knew, relay his conversation with Vera to Detective Chief Inspector Rodgers. After all, she had freely admitted that both she and Alice had hated Gunilla – Alice from jealousy, herself from heartless rejection. They had both certainly had a motive, even though Vera had denied that either of them had anything to do with the Swedish girl's death. But the Inspector was most unlikely to be interested; as far as he was concerned the case was virtually closed.

For once, Ester Simmons was not working in her garden. Passing her cottage, he saw that the door was shut, though windows were open. She, at least, had not entrusted him with her secret – whatever it was.

On an impulse, he went up to the front door and knocked. After a while, she opened it, looking startled. He lifted his cap to her.

'I'm so sorry to disturb you,' he said. 'But I wanted to ask you the name of those charming blue flowers by your gate.'

'They're blue poppies,' she said. '*Meconopsis grandis,* if you want the Latin name.'

He smiled at her. 'Plain English will do. Are they hard to grow?'

'I've never had any trouble. I divide the clump every two or three years and they don't seem to mind.'

'Well, they're very attractive. I'll remember the name.'

She hesitated. 'You're welcome to come in for a cup of coffee, if you like, Colonel.'

'If it's not too much trouble.'

'Not at all. I seldom get visitors these days. It'll make a pleasant change.'

He went into a narrow hallway, which Hans Birger would certainly have eliminated, and followed her into the sitting room.

It reminded him of Miss Butler's front room at Lupin Cottage, which had the same air of impoverished gentility, but it was nothing like as pin-neat nor as spotlessly clean. Freda Butler

145

would have been shocked by the old ashes lingering in the fire grate, the unpolished brass fender, by the layer of dust and the disorder.

He waited while Ester Simmons went off to make the tea, looking round the room with curiosity. In his experience, photographs put out on display often provided interesting clues to their owner – as in the case of Miss Butler's fearsome father, the Admiral, who glared down from the top of a bureau. But here there was only a faded studio portrait of a nondescript couple in Edwardian clothing and another of a young woman wearing a nurse's uniform – the proper old-fashioned kind of uniform with frilled and starched cap and cuffs. He would have expected to see several photos of Miss Simmons seated in the centre of rows of village schoolchildren, but there was nothing of the kind. He was looking at the nurse again when Ester Simmons came back carrying a tray with two cups of coffee.

'My late sister,' she said. 'She trained at Guy's Hospital in London. She died before she was thirty. Cancer.'

'How sad. I'm sorry.'

'It was a long, long time ago. I find it extraordinary to think that while she has never grown old, I'm now in my eighties. I wonder what it would be like for us to meet again? Like two strangers, I suppose. If there's such a thing as the afterlife, I can't imagine how that sort of oddity is sorted out. Do you believe in life after death, Colonel?'

'I'm afraid not.'

'Don't worry, nor do I. To be honest, I hope there isn't one. The mere idea is exhausting.'

'Were you close to your sister?'

'Very. We shared rather a miserable childhood. Our parents believed in strict discipline and not sparing the rod. Come to that, so do I. I suppose I must have inherited from them. I can't stand all the mollycoddling and nonsense that goes on today. Parents blaming teachers for correcting their spoiled children's appalling behaviour. Child psychiatrists making up all sorts of ridiculous excuses for it. Children getting away with murder. There's nothing wrong with a bit of corporal punishment in my view, if it's deserved.' She set the tray down on a low table. 'Do you take sugar?'

The cups and saucers, he realized, had exactly the same pattern as those used by the Frog End Women's Institute to serve teas at local functions, including the annual summer fête. For some reason, he felt a pang of homesickness.

He said, 'The police don't seem to have made much progress in finding Gunilla Bjork's killer, do they?'

'I didn't expect them to.'

'Do you have any thoughts yourself?'

'Thoughts, Colonel?'

'You knew the girl, and what she was like. I remember you describing her as Trouble with a capital T.'

'That's right. She was.'

'And you disliked her very much?'

'Yes, I certainly did. And I wasn't alone in that, I might add. At first, I felt rather sorry for her. You see, I occasionally used to have pupils at my school who were rather similar. There was always some fundamental flaw in their make-up or some happening in their background that was not their fault and I found that it could never be eradicated. In my opinion, Gunilla fell into that category. But there was also something quite evil about her. She enjoyed the harm and suffering she caused. It amused her very much.'

'Did you come across her at the Golden Pheasant?'

'I don't go to pubs, Colonel. I don't drink.'

'But you saw enough of her to know what she was like?'

'Oh, yes. I knew what she was like. She used to walk by this house on her way to and from the village shop. She had a sweet tooth, you see, and she was very fond of Alice's cakes. As I told you, Vera was very smitten with her. Besotted is the word. Poor Alice was extremely upset.'

'So I gather.'

'The shop is a hotbed for gossip, of course, but I hardly ever go there myself – it's too expensive for me. I go to a supermarket in town instead, once a month in my old car.'

'You hear all the gossip, nonetheless?'

'It comes to me, Colonel. I spend a lot of time working in my garden and people often stop to talk at my gate as they pass by. They don't like me much, but they use me as a sort of listening post. I hear most of what's going on in the village.'

'Did Gunilla ever stop to talk to you?'

'No. I was of no interest to her. But, one day, when she was going past, I stopped *her* and told her exactly what I thought about her behaviour.'

'And what did she say?'

'She said I was a frustrated old maid and told me to mind my own business.' Miss Simmons stirred her coffee briskly. 'There was another occasion when she spoke to me, Colonel. I may as well tell you about it. I know I can trust your discretion.'

For the second time in a single day his discretion was on the line.

'Of course.'

'Some time later, when she came by, she called me over to the gate. I thought at first that she might be going to apologize for her rudeness but, of course, she wasn't. Instead, she said that she had something to tell me. Something I ought to know.'

'What was that?'

'She told me that a man had come into the Golden Pheasant who had been one of my pupils at the village school, many years ago. She said that he'd told her all about how I'd beaten him until he bled and that I'd taken a perverted pleasure in it. He said that I'd done the same to other children in the school as well but they were all too frightened to tell anyone. Then she said that she was going to tell all the people in the village because they should know how wicked I was.'

'And what did you say?'

'I told her to do what she damned well liked. I told her nobody would believe a word of it and that she'd made the whole thing up. Of course,

149

she laughed at me – the same way she laughed at everybody. It wasn't me that was wicked, Colonel, it was her.'

'What happened, then?'

'She disappeared.' Ester Simmons gave him a dry look. 'And I don't deny that I was extremely glad to see the back of her. But that doesn't mean that I murdered her. I can assure you that I didn't.'

Crispin Fellows might have been on the right track, he thought. Caning children had been common enough in those days; six of the best had been perfectly normal. But perverted pleasure taken in it was a different matter altogether.

'You do believe me, don't you, Colonel?'

'Yes, of course.'

But he wasn't sure if he did. Or if he didn't.

Thirteen

Cornelia was having lunch with a friend, which gave the Colonel a perfect excuse to stop at the Golden Pheasant to sample some more of their home cooking and Edward Maplin's ale. Sausage and mash was on the menu: a good old English dish, the kind he liked best.

He ordered it from Kevin and took his pint over to the corner table where he had sat before. Betty Turner brought a mat, cutlery and a proper napkin.

'Nice to see you again, sir. You're getting to be quite a regular.'

He smiled. 'Not for much longer, I'm afraid.'

'Well, I'm sure Mrs Heathcote's been very thankful to have your help.' She moved a step closer and lowered her voice. 'The police came to ask me more questions.'

'Oh?'

'They wanted to know if I knew what Gunilla's suitcase looked like.'

'Do you?'

'Well, I only went into her room a couple of times and I can't really remember. It was dark blue, I think, and cheap, like cardboard. Anyway, it was gone when I came back from helping with my grandson. There wasn't anything at all left of Gunilla's in the room. Nothing. I know that because Mrs Barton asked me to give it a good clean. I was amazed that Gunilla had cleared it out so thoroughly, considering how lazy and messy she always was, and with her leaving in such a hurry. Mrs Barton told me she went the same day that Mr Barton gave her the sack. Couldn't wait to be out of the place.'

'What did Mrs Barton think of Gunilla?'

'I don't know. She never said. She always kept her opinions to herself. I suppose she had to put up with her, seeing that she couldn't help her husband like he needed. Not that Gunilla ever did much work. Between you and me, I think Mr Barton only hired her in the first place because he thought she'd be good for business. The pub hadn't been doing too well before Gunilla arrived on the scene. Once word got around about her, everything changed and the customers were flocking in.'

'How did Mr Barton treat her?'

'Well, he'd be angry with her when she hadn't done something she was supposed to do, but she'd get away with it, every time. She'd peep round her hair at him, like she did with all the others, and she'd laugh at him.' Mrs Turner gave the linen napkin a tweak. 'Of course, men are all the same.'

The Colonel rather hoped that he was included in this sweeping statement; it would be nice to know that, for once, he was not considered entirely trustworthy.

'Do you mean Mr Barton was attracted by Gunilla?'

'Oh yes. He didn't show it – he wasn't that kind of man – but I could tell that he was. And

152

she'd have known it. She flirted with him, like she did with all the rest. Of course, she was just leading him on. Playing her games. He wouldn't have been at all her type.'

'What exactly was her type?'

'Hard to say. But she liked them to be a bit of fun.'

'And Mr Barton wasn't fun?'

'He was overworked, poor man – running a pub's a very hard job – and there was always Mrs Barton's health to worry about. I felt sorry for him.'

The sausage and mash, when it came, was accompanied by a rich onion gravy and mushy peas. And, praise God, Betty Turner even remembered the Colman's English mustard.

Afterwards, he walked on towards the house, thinking over what Betty Turner had told him. Inspector Rodgers had dismissed the Bartons as of no consequence to the investigation: Mrs Barton being a sick old lady and Mr Barton beyond communication in his grave. The Colonel was not so sure he agreed. The Bartons could hold the key to what had happened to Gunilla. And why.

He arrived at the house at the same time as Cornelia returned in the Range Rover from her lunch. She was in high spirits and he realized that she was rather drunk.

'Pour me a brandy, will you, Hugh? I feel like celebrating.'

He fetched the decanter and a glass, poured the five star brandy and lit her cigarette.

'What are you celebrating, Cornelia?'

'Getting rid of this bloody place. Henry Willoughby called me to say they've already got someone interested.'

'That's fast.'

'Well, they know what they're doing. He's bringing them here tomorrow. They're Dutch, apparently. They grow tulips in a big way. I don't care if they're Hottentots so long as they buy it.' She took a gulp at the glass. 'Won't you join me, Hugh?'

'No, thanks.'

'Well, sit down, at least. Don't just stand there. My God, I'll be rid of Gunilla Bjork at last! I can forget all about that horrible bitch.'

He said, 'Not quite yet. Her murder hasn't been solved.'

'And it probably won't be, will it? How can the police ever find out? It's been too long. Too late. They don't care anyway. Nobody does. She wasn't worth caring about.'

He watched her take another gulp. 'You never told me about the Bartons, Cornelia.'

'Who?'

'The couple who employed Gunilla at the Golden Pheasant.'

'Oh, *them*. What about them? There was nothing to tell except that they weren't very good at running a pub, poor things. In fact, they were useless. You've got to know what you're doing these days – like Henry Willoughby.'

'Apparently, Roy Barton fell for Gunilla.'

'Well, I expect he did. I mean, there she was flaunting herself like crazy and he had an invalid wife . . . Of course he did. But Gunilla wouldn't

154

have bothered with him, except to tease him. He was a very dreary sort of man.'

'No fun?'

'No fun at all. And she liked fun, God rot her! Well, she did rot, didn't she? Down to her bones.' Cornelia emptied her glass. 'I think I'll go and lie down for a bit, Hugh.'

'That's not a bad idea.'

She started up the circular staircase, clinging with both hands to the steel rail, and he called after her.

'By the way, I'll be out tomorrow.'

She stopped and turned round. 'All day?'

'Yes, all day.'

'But you'll be back by the evening?'

'I should think so.'

'Where are you going, Hugh?'

He said firmly, 'That's my business, Cornelia.'

He took the scenic route to Poole, across country, and stopped at a small pub for some lunch. Neither the beer, nor the food was a patch on what the Golden Pheasant provided but it was a friendly place and he was able to sit outside in the sun.

A phone call ahead to the General Hospital at Poole had confirmed that Mrs Maureen Barton was a patient there and that afternoon visiting was allowed between three and four thirty p.m. To kill time, he went down to the harbour and watched the sailing boats coming and going on the water and breathed in the salty air.

He could understand why Alice and Vera were attracted by the idea of living by the sea. If he

155

had been a navy man, he might have done so himself instead of retiring to a landlocked village. As Vera had rightly said, there was something clean and honest about it, and he also felt that it imparted a kind of mysterious solace to the soul. A panacea for all troubles. Fortunately in England, the sea was never very far away. It was always there to commune with, if one felt the need.

He returned to the hospital and followed the signs for the ward.

At its entrance, he asked a nurse where he could find Mrs Barton. She was nothing like Miss Simmons's sister in the photograph. No starched cap or apron, just a shapeless nylon overall.

She frowned. 'You're not another of those CID people, are you?'

'Definitely not.'

'Because the one that came before upset her.'

'I promise that I won't.'

'She hardly says anything. And she wouldn't talk to the police sergeant at all. Not a word.'

'Perhaps I might have better luck.'

She assessed him with a professional glance. 'Well, she doesn't have any other visitors, poor old thing, so you might cheer her up a bit.'

'How is she?'

She turned down a thumb. 'There's not a lot we can do except keep her as comfortable as possible.'

Maureen Barton was in a separate room nearest the ward entrance. Laura had been in a similar room: a place for patients who needed extra care and attention and who were not expected to live long.

She was lying motionless, eyes shut, and surrounded by the monitors and apparatus that were keeping her alive. A small, frail woman, as pale as death.

He sat down on a chair by the head of the bed, which brought him down to her level. When he spoke her name, she opened her eyes.

'Mrs Barton,' he said. 'I've come to talk about Gunilla Bjork – if you don't mind.'

There was no response but, eventually, she turned her head slowly in his direction. When she answered, her voice was weak: not more than a whisper.

'I don't know you. Who are you?'

He gave her his name.

'I've been staying in King's Mowbray with Mrs Heathcote, an old friend of my late wife. She and her husband bought the farm that used to belong to the Holland family. You may remember them coming to the Golden Pheasant?'

'Mr Heathcote came all the time . . . I never liked him.'

He said, 'You would remember Gunilla Bjork, too. She worked for you and your husband, didn't she?'

Her lips moved slowly. 'She was no good . . . Roy had to give her the sack.'

'So I understand.' He paused. 'Gunilla's remains were found recently, buried in the Hollands' old barn. The Heathcotes' builders came across her skeleton when they were working there.'

She turned her head away from him, shut her eyes again.

'I'm not a policeman, Mrs Barton,' he said.

'But I'm here because I think that your late husband may have had something to do with Gunilla's death.'

After a moment, her eyes reopened.

'He didn't kill her, if that's what you mean.'

'Will you tell me what happened?'

'Why do you want to know?'

Why indeed, he wondered. There was no good reason, except perhaps that a Chief Detective Inspector in thrall to a Greek goddess could not be expected to care very much about the death of a Swedish barmaid. It seemed important that someone did.

'I'd like to know the truth.'

She was silent for several minutes, then she sighed.

'I might as well. Nobody can do anything about it now. Roy's dead and I'll be gone soon.'

He waited and, presently, she went on. Her voice was even fainter and he had to bend his head close to hear her words.

'I knew it was a mistake . . . hiring a girl like. She was bone lazy and nothing but trouble from the first . . . flirting with all the men . . . they were like bees round a honeypot.'

'So I've heard.'

'She'd tease them . . . lead them on . . . tempt them. I never thought Roy would fall for it . . . but he did. Just like all the rest. I knew by the way he looked at her. I couldn't blame him . . . I hadn't been a proper wife to him for years – not since I got so ill. He couldn't help himself. Poor Roy. He was a good man.'

He said quietly, 'Tell me about it.'

'Gunilla used to go to the Hollands' barn . . . to meet men. She'd play a silly make-believe thing . . . pretending to be a prisoner up in the hayloft and they'd have to climb up the ladder to rescue her.'

'How did you know this?'

'Some of them bragged about it in the bar. And Roy told me himself . . . afterwards.'

'What did he tell you exactly?'

'He said he followed her to the barn one afternoon. She was on her own, he said . . . she didn't go to meet anyone that time. He watched her climb up the ladder to the hayloft and lie down with her hair hanging over the side, playing that game of hers. Some sort of old fairy tale.'

'And then?'

'She caught sight of Roy. She teased him, like she always teased them all . . . said if he climbed all the way up, he could have her as a reward. He was fit enough then, so it wasn't difficult for him . . . but when he got to the top she wouldn't let him near her. Told him he disgusted her and she'd sooner be dead than have him touch her, and she'd tell me that he'd tried to rape her. She made him so angry that he put his hands round her throat. He swore he didn't mean to hurt her . . . that he let her go at once.'

'Did you believe him?'

'Yes. I know he was telling me the truth. He said she got into a terrible panic and rushed to climb down the ladder, but somehow she slipped and fell. When he reached her, he found the back of her head had hit a flint stone. She was dead.'

'Why didn't he report the accident to the police?'

'There were red marks round her throat from his hands . . . he said they'd never believe he hadn't killed her with the stone . . . never believe it was an accident. He thought he'd be arrested and tried for murder.'

'So, he buried her in the barn?'

'He dug a hole with the flint stone – they're sharp, you know, they make good tools. It wasn't very deep but it was enough to hide her. We didn't think she'd ever be found.'

She might well not have been, the Colonel thought, if it hadn't been for Cornelia's bright idea of having a sprung dance floor.

'What about her belongings?'

'We put them all in her suitcase. Roy got rid of it in a pond miles away from King's Mowbray.'

'And the flint stone?'

'He threw it into a stream. We told everyone that Roy had given her the sack and that she'd packed and left. Most of them were glad, you know . . . she'd upset too many people.'

He was silent for a moment.

Maureen Barton was looking at him. 'You must do what you think best, Colonel. Tell the police, if you want. I don't care now. It doesn't matter any more. Roy and I never had children and there's no other family left.'

She turned her head away.

He clasped her hand before he stood up and moved quietly towards the door.

She spoke again, quite clearly.

'Roy was in the army, like you, Colonel

– before we started with the pub. He was in the Devon and Dorsets. He always said they were the best years of his life. You'd understand that.'

'Yes,' he said. 'Indeed, I do.'

'He was a good man.'

'I'm sure he was.'

As he left the ward, the same nurse accosted him.

'I hope you didn't upset her.'

'No,' he said. 'As a matter of fact, I think she was quite glad to talk to me.'

The Colonel drove back to King's Mowbray, taking his time. Maureen Barton had believed her husband's story without question; he wasn't quite so sure that he did and he doubted that Detective Chief Inspector Rodgers, with his sardonic reference to fairy tales, would have believed a word of it. *You must do what you think best. Tell the police, if you want. It doesn't matter any more.*

He had been in a similarly tricky situation before, where someone guilty of a crime had confided in him. This one was no easier. The truth always mattered, but sometimes it could never be known. Or need never be known. Whatever had happened, Roy Barton was beyond the reach of the law, and so was his dying wife. And nothing could restore Gunilla Bjork to her uncaring family. Nor did there seem much point in hampering Chief Inspector Rodgers's steady progress towards a blissful retirement with his irises.

The Range Rover was parked outside the house

161

and he found Cornelia sitting on the sofa, drink in hand. Her third, at least, he reckoned, by the look of her.

'Come and join me, Hugh. I need cheering up.'

He fetched a whisky. 'What's the trouble?'

'Howard's coming home in two days.'

'Isn't that a cause for celebration?'

'Not exactly. He's in a foul mood about everything. You'd think that finding the skeleton was all my fault. As though I'd put the bloody thing there myself, just to annoy him.'

He smiled. 'I know that you didn't, Cornelia.'

'Nice of you to be so sure, Hugh. We'll probably never find out who did, will we?'

'I shouldn't think so.'

'Anyway, who cares? Howard refuses to come down here any more, so I'll be going back to London. Good riddance to the place!'

He'd be glad to be rid of it himself.

'What about the Swiss couple? Aren't they arriving soon?'

'They'll come to London with me. I don't suppose they'll mind. They're being paid enough.' She raised her glass to him unsteadily. 'Thanks for everything, Hugh. I'll miss you most terribly. You've been a wonderful comfort and I couldn't have managed without you.'

'I'm glad to have been of help.'

'Oh, by the way, I almost forgot . . . some woman phoned for you. She said she was your next-door neighbour. Voice like a foghorn.'

'Did she leave a message?'

'She wanted you to call her. Something about a cat.'

Fourteen

Damn! Damn! Damn! He should never have left Thursday for so long. He should have gone home days ago instead of playing at being Sherlock Holmes, as well as cook/companion/comforter to Cornelia who, whatever she pretended, could have managed perfectly well without him.

'*Now?*' she'd said, looking at him as though he'd gone mad. 'You're rushing back to Dorset for a *cat*?'

'Yes, Cornelia, I am. For a cat.'

'Can't it wait till morning?'

'No, it can't.'

'But what about me?'

'You'll be fine,' he'd said, knowing that she would be.

When he had rung Naomi, she had sounded breezily cheerful.

'Just thought I'd better let you know, Hugh. Thursday hasn't been around for three days. I've had a search through the house and the garden and kept calling him, but no luck so far. I shouldn't worry too much, he'll come back when it suits him.'

That was just the trouble, the Colonel thought. If Thursday took it into his head that he'd been deserted, then it wouldn't at all suit him to come back. He'd move on, just as he would have moved on throughout his long cat life, which must have included some very hard times. Thursday was like Kipling's cat that walked by himself, and all places were alike to him.

He drove much faster than his usual pace, taking corners at a lick, roaring down the straight bits. The Riley responded as though it understood the urgency. It was still light when the Colonel arrived back in Frog End, the summer evening fading towards dusk. The food that Naomi had left out lay untouched in the bowl marked DOG beside the kitchen door. He went out and walked down to the far end of the garden, calling the cat's name, hoping that he would suddenly make an appearance. He even checked the padlocked shed which he noticed bore distinct signs of Naomi's inquisitive presence with the excuse of the mower. Tins and jars not put back in their proper place, the work stool slightly askew. After that, he searched the cottage from top to bottom, opening cupboard doors, looking under beds, behind furniture, on window seats, anywhere that Thursday might conceivably be curled up asleep.

When he rang Naomi, she answered almost at once.

'Saw your car outside, Hugh. Any luck?'

'I'm afraid not.'

'I'm very sorry about it. I feel it's my fault.'

She sounded upset and he said quickly, 'Of course it wasn't, Naomi. It's entirely *my* fault for leaving him for too long. It was stupid of me.'

'Well, he'll probably come back as soon as he realizes you're home again. You know how cats are . . . they've got a sixth sense, besides the nine lives.'

164

He didn't really know how cats were, never having owned one, and he certainly didn't own Thursday. For some mysterious reason, the battle-scarred old warrior, down on his luck, had chosen to throw in his lot with him – subject to satisfaction, of course, which he had signally failed to provide.

'I hope you're right.'

'By the way, what happened about the skeleton in the barn?'

'The police took it away. They're still investigating. Somehow, I don't think they'll ever solve the mystery.'

'Why not?'

He shrugged. 'No hard evidence. Nothing for them to go on. It had been there for six years.'

'Did they find out the cause of death?'

'You're sounding ghoulish, Naomi.'

'Well, it's a ghoulish story. Did they?'

'She died from a blow to the skull.'

'She?'

'It turned out that the skeleton belonged to a young Swedish girl who had worked at the local pub. Apparently, she was in the habit of meeting admirers in the barn.'

'Well, there you are.'

'Where am I, Naomi?'

'One of them killed her. That's obvious.'

'You may well be right.'

'Of course I'm right. Even the police, slow as they are, ought to have worked out which one by now. You always seem to be getting mixed up with dead women, Hugh. First Ursula Swynford, then that actress – whatever her name was – then this foreign girl. I don't know how you do it.'

'I don't do anything.'

'It could become a habit.'

'I'll see if I can make it a man next time.'

'That would be a change. How's your friend, by the way? It must have been jolly unpleasant for her. Nobody wants a body to turn up in the barn.'

'She's getting over it. Her husband's due back from his business trip soon.'

'I was afraid she might get her hooks into you.'

He smiled. 'Yes, I know you were. There was no likelihood of that, I can assure you, Naomi. I'm not in her league.'

She snorted. 'Take a good look in the mirror some time, Hugh.'

He rang off and went out into the garden again. The light was going fast. Soon it would be too dark to see. He fetched a torch and did another patrol, poking about among bushes with a stick. He remembered reading an article about old lions always going off to die alone in a hidden place. If small cats were the same as big cats, then Thursday could have done the same. He might never be found.

Finally, he went back into the cottage, switched on the sitting room lamps, poured himself a large whisky and sat down in the wing-back tapestry chair by the inglenook. The sofa opposite was where Thursday spent a great deal of his time, especially in winter when the log fire was lit. It looked bare without the customary ball of black and tan fur, and the house felt depressingly empty.

When the telephone rang, he got up wearily to answer it.

'Hallo, Father.'

He could tell from his daughter-in-law's agitated tone that he was in deep trouble.

'How are you, Susan?'

'We've been very worried about you, Father . . . where on earth have you been? We've tried ringing you ever so many times but there's never any answer.' Her voice was even louder than Naomi's at her worst. 'We were thinking of calling the police.'

'I've been away,' he said. 'Staying with a friend.'

'You ought to have told us, then we wouldn't have worried.'

'There was no need to worry. I do go away sometimes, you know.'

'Will you be sure to tell us, in future?'

He suppressed his irritation, knowing that she meant well. 'I'll try to remember.'

'How are you, then?'

'Perfectly well, thank you. How are you all?'

'Well, Eric's got over his cold but Edith's caught it now.'

'I'm sorry about that. I hope you and Marcus didn't catch it too.'

'No, but we're both very tired. Edith's been very chesty and waking up a lot at night. We have to take it in turns to sit with her.'

He sympathized, remembering the nights when he and Laura had done the same with Alison and Marcus when they were ill. 'She'll get over it soon.'

'I hope so. Have you had your supper, Father?'

'Yes,' he lied.

'Did you try the pasta?'

'Not yet.'

'Are you taking those multivitamin pills we sent you?'

He had no compunction in lying again. 'Yes, indeed.'

'They're very important for your health.'

'Yes, I know.'

'Especially at your age.'

'I'm aware of that.'

She changed tack abruptly, veering on to another course. 'Who did you go and stay with?'

'An old friend.'

'Oh?'

He knew that she wanted to know more. Was the old friend a woman, and, if so, was she a widow or a divorcee and therefore, in Susan's eyes, a potential predator? As she had once pointed out to him, he had to be careful. Careful of what? he had asked innocently and much to her discomfort. He had no intention of satisfying her curiosity this time, or any other.

'Well, thank you for ringing, Susan. I'm just off to bed.'

'Oh . . .' The wind was temporarily out of her sails but she came around fast. 'By the way, that nice bungalow down the road that I told you about is still on the market. You really ought to come and view it, Father. It would be much better if you were living near us.'

'I'll bear it in mind.'

He returned to his whisky, and when it was

finished, he poured the other half. He had no appetite for any supper and no desire to go to bed, in spite of what he had told his daughter-in-law. He slept better now, but the nights still held too many wakeful hours and too many remembered memories and regrets.

After a while, he put on one of his old Gilbert and Sullivan records and sat listening as Mabel sang from *The Pirates of Penzance.*

Poor wandering one!
Though thou hast surely strayed,
Take heart of grace,
Thy steps retrace,
Poor wandering one!

He could only hope that Thursday would do likewise.

During the next two days, the Colonel kept busy. Jacob had cut the lawn in his absence, but there was plenty to be done in the flower beds – weeding, staking, deadheading, trimming, and the white lavender that Naomi had looked after needed to be planted. The irises beside the pond were looking happy with their damp feet and he admired their tall branched stems of beautiful golden-yellow flowers. He could see what attracted Detective Chief Inspector Rodgers.

The terrace was also looking good and growing some rather nice moss, but garden chairs were needed if it were to fulfil its function. Naomi had suggested a place to look for them locally and he followed her advice and found just what he wanted – sturdy things made of a wood that would weather to silver-grey and look right with the old flagstones. He also bought a matching table for the sundowner drinks. All to be delivered the next day. On his way home, he stopped at a pet shop and bought some Cats' Treats. *Shake the pouch*, the makers promised, *and watch your cat come running!* He thought that most unlikely. Thursday was not some performing circus animal or interested in pleasing humans.

He kept on patrolling the garden and hunted in the ditches along the road outside the cottage in case Thursday had been hit by a car, but, to his relief, there was no sad, wet bundle of black and tan fur.

Ruth Swynford phoned.

'Naomi told me that Thursday's gone missing?'

'I'm afraid so.'

'I've spread the word round. Somebody might spot him.'

'Thank you, Ruth. That's kind of you.'

'I expect he'll come back on his own.'

He'd given up expecting any such thing. 'How are the wedding plans going?'

'Chaotic. I'm thinking of backing out.'

He hoped that she was joking, knowing that she had had cold feet about accepting Tom Harvey. There had been a long and unhappy love affair with a married man before the young doctor had so fortuitously arrived on the scene. Then she laughed.

'Don't worry, I'm only joking. I hope you're still going to give me away, Colonel?'

170

'It will be an honour and I'm looking forward to it very much.' Both statements were more than true.

'Almost the whole village is coming, so it should be fun. Let's pray the weather's kind to us.'

Ah, the unavoidable lottery of the English summer! Weddings, fêtes, school sports, garden parties, barbecues, open air plays and concerts all depending on the whim of the weather. He hoped the sun would shine for Ruth and Tom. They deserved it.

Major Cuthbertson was at the bar of the Dog and Duck when he strolled over for a lunchtime pint. He seemed somewhat taken aback to see him.

'Thought you were away, Colonel.'

'Yes, I was.'

'Heard you'd probably be gone for some time.'

'No. I'm back now. What will you have, Major?'

'Very good of you. A whisky, if you don't mind.'

'A double for the Major, Bill.'

The Dog and Duck's landlord had none of the professional slickness of the Golden Pheasant's Kevin, and Crispin Fellows would abhor the patterned carpeting, the cheap glint of modern copper and brass and the synthetic shine of plastic, not to mention the unexceptional beer and the microwaved food. But there were at least a dozen people in the bar who had spent most of their lives in the village and one old man sitting with his dog in the corner who had never been out of it.

The Major raised his double whisky. 'Good

171

health, Colonel. I take it you're recovered from that bad dose of flu you had?'

'Yes, thank you.'

'No lasting effects?'

'None whatever.'

'We can't be too careful at our age.'

He forbore to point out that he was actually several years younger than the Major.

'No, indeed.'

'Feeling up to snuff, then?'

The Major was looking at him as though he very much hoped he wasn't and the Colonel suddenly remembered Miss Butler's little bird who had spread the word that the Major had felt himself to be the obvious choice to give Ruth away at her wedding.

It would be kindest, the Colonel thought, not to give him any false hopes.

'I'm in excellent health at the moment, thank you.'

'Jolly good!' The Major conceded defeat and changed the subject. 'Did you hear there's going to be a rounders match on the green? *Rounders,* for God's sake! A girls' game! What'll they think of next?'

'Baseball?'

'*Baseball!* The bloody Yanks play that.'

'It's rather similar and I believe it's getting quite popular over here.'

The Major shook his head fiercely. 'I don't know what this country's coming to. All these damn fool modern ideas. The village green's meant for cricket, and *only* cricket. Everybody knows that.'

Back in the cottage, the Colonel sat down in

the wing-chair with the latest parish magazine and flicked through the pages. There were the usual announcements for club meetings, coffee mornings, jumble sales, a talk, with slides, on someone's visit to Katmandu, details of recent weddings and funerals and a notice about the proposed Rounders on the Green that had so appalled the Major. Several gardens were to be opened for charity and the Twinning Association had held a pétanque party for their opposite numbers visiting from France. A monthly lunch club had been started up and the proposed menu for the next meeting was cottage pie and vegetables, followed by fruit trifle. The forthcoming village fête, of which he was treasurer, was given a whole page. As usual, there would be cake, plant, bottle and bric-a-brac stalls, as well as pony rides, cream teas, quoits, a guess-the-weight cake and a grand raffle – all to the accompaniment of a silver band. And, something quite new to him – a duck race. Who on the committee had put that novel idea forward? Certainly not the Major.

The magazine advertisements were always intriguing. A funeral service offered prepayment plans (pay now, die later?) a builder made yurts to order (whatever yurts were), a local photographer's credentials proclaimed: *Shoots Everything.*

He wondered if King's Mowbray produced a parish magazine and, if so, what it would be like. Rather different, he thought. The residents were unlikely to be interested in other people's cast-offs, or in amateur slide shows, or in opening their landscaped gardens to the general public.

He put down the magazine and his mind went

back again to the Wiltshire village, to the old barn and to the death of Gunilla Bjork.

You must do what you think best. So far as he could still see, after a good deal of thought and soul-searching over days, the best thing was to do nothing. Maureen Barton would be left to die in peace; Detective Chief Inspector Rodgers would retire happily to his irises; and King's Mowbray would soon forget all about the troublesome, heartless Swedish girl. The police investigation would soon be closed for lack of any leads and the file put away to gather dust with all the other unsolved cases, just as DCI Rodgers had predicted.

He had told Maureen Barton that he had wanted to know the truth and she had given it to him, as she believed it. Gunilla's fall to her death had been an accident, her husband had not meant to harm her. He had been a good man, according to her.

On impulse, he lifted the phone and called DCI Rodgers.

'Any developments yet, Inspector?'

'Not a thing, Colonel.'

'By the way, I went to see Mrs Barton in hospital.'

'Oh? Why did you do that?'

'I just thought she might have something to say. In a lucid moment.'

'And did she?'

'Nothing that would make much difference.'

'Don't waste your time any more, Colonel. This is our job.'

'No,' he said slowly. 'I won't.'

174

Fifteen

He must have drifted off to sleep because the next thing he heard was the sound of the grandfather clock striking five, and when he opened his eyes he saw Thursday sitting in the doorway, watching him.

He said, not daring to move, 'Hallo, old chap. Nice to have you back again.'

The cat's gaze was unblinking and unforgiving. A basilisk stare.

The Colonel understood the form. Humble obeisance was required. A respectful distance kept. Repentance clearly demonstrated.

He got up and walked past the cat and on into the kitchen. In the cupboard he found a tin of sardines intended for human consumption (his). He emptied the fish into the clean bowl marked DOG, set it down on the floor and waited. He knew better than to insult the cat by shaking the pouch of Cats' Treats.

After what seemed like a very long time, Thursday appeared and stalked huffily towards the dish. The Colonel held his breath. Sardines, he knew, were a particular favourite and not often on the menu. The cat stopped to sniff the air from a distance, turned away, and then turned back again to approach closer. More sniffing and more hesitation before he finally crouched down on his haunches and began to eat.

The Colonel breathed a deep sigh of relief.
He went to phone Naomi.

'He's back.'

'Thank heavens for that, Hugh! I was beginning
to get worried.'

'So was I. Come round and celebrate. The
sundowner terrace has chairs and is officially
open.'

'I'll be there at six.'

'Earlier, if you can make it.'

'I'll come now. By the way, Hugh, have you
realized today's Thursday?'

When he opened the front door to her, she was
wearing the furry white tracksuit that always
reminded him of a polar bear, her moon boot
trainers and an enormous hat on her head – an
elaborate creation, garnished with an assortment
of flowers and feathers, and trimmed with a gauzy
veil that covered her face and finished in a large
bow under her chin.

'My wedding hat,' she said, enlightening him.
'For Ruth and Tom. I was trying it on. Wondered
what you'd think of it.'

'Magnificent,' he said, gallantly and truthfully.
'Where did you buy it?'

'I didn't *buy* it anywhere. I found it in the trunk
up in the loft. I think it must have belonged to
my Great-Aunt Rosalind. It's Edwardian, of
course.'

The same trunk had already produced an
impressive wolf-fur hat and her grandfather's
Canadian lumberjack's cap. He wondered what
other treasures it contained.

He led the way through the kitchen and out on

176

to the terrace where the sun was playing its part to set the scene. The new furniture looked good and so did the decanter and glasses placed ready on the table, with a jug of water for Naomi's splash. She settled herself comfortably while he poured their drinks.

'This is very nice, Hugh. What a good idea of mine!'

'Yes, it was.'

'Where's Thursday?'

'Fast asleep on the sofa. I'm still in the doghouse but I think he's coming round to giving me the benefit of the doubt.'

'No ill effects?'

'He's a bit stiff and dusty, but otherwise he seems fine.'

'Extraordinary that he came back today, of all days.'

'Yes, wasn't it? He obviously knows the days of the week.' He handed her her glass, sat down and raised his own to her.

'To many more sundowners, Naomi.'

'I'll second that.' She tried drinking through the veil, without success, untied the bow and flung it back over the hat. 'This stupid thing. I don't know how women managed in those days.'

It was very pleasant sitting in the gentle warmth of the evening sun, watching it sink gradually beyond the trees, and with a full glass in hand. Naomi had been quite right.

He said, 'So, tell me about the fête committee that I missed.'

'Well, you're rather in the doghouse with

Madame Chairman as well, but, I dare say, she'll come round too, like Thursday.'

'Did the meeting go all right?'

'If you call lasting for nearly three hours going all right. There was the usual pitched battle of the trestle tables, with the Major and Mrs Bentley almost coming to blows. Marjorie had to put a stop to it in the end. I really don't know why she lets the Major run the bottle stall – it's like putting a fox in charge of chickens. Philippa Rankin's down to one pony for the rides, which is a shame, and there was a big argument over the teas and what to charge this year. Ruth was present, of course, and she's a jolly good sport about everything. Doesn't mind us selling ice creams or having a pet show for the children. Not a bit difficult like her mother used to be.'

'I read in the magazine that there's to be a duck race.'

Naomi chuckled. 'Mrs Warner put that forward – she'd seen one at some other fête. It should be a hoot. Then somebody else suggested a samba band instead of the silver one we always have – you should have heard what the Major had to say about that. Damned foreign rubbish, he called it! Anyway, Marjorie shot the whole idea down in flames.'

The Colonel smiled. No English summer fête would be complete without the sound of a band – silver or brass – and its faltering version of *Born Free* and *The Dam Busters*. The pulsating, exotic rhythms of South America would strike all the wrong notes. He rather agreed with the Major.

178

'I'm looking forward to it.'

'Well, let's hope nobody gets murdered this year.' Naomi waved her glass at the garden. 'It's all looking pretty good, Hugh. Lots still to be done, but you're making real progress.'

This was praise indeed.

'The white lavender seems to have settled in well.'

'So I see. It shimmers at dusk, you know, and it's got a wonderful smell. Sweeter than the purple kind. Bumble bees love it.' She wagged a stern finger at him. 'You have to be tough with it, though, Hugh. Eight, eight, eight. That's the golden rule.'

'Three eights?'

'You have to cut it back on the eighth day of the eighth month, down to eight inches. Rather like Armistice Day. Cut it into a hedgehog shape, then you'll get it to grow right.'

'I'll remember,' he promised. 'Many thanks for all you did in the garden while I was away.'

'I just threw some water over anything that needed it and pulled out a few weeds. By the way, you had some enchanter's nightshade in the far corner so I got rid of that for you. Took all the roots out and burned them.'

'That sounds rather drastic.'

'I can assure you there's nothing enchanting about enchanter's nightshade except its white flowers. It's a weed and a bloody nuisance. Runs sideways everywhere, if you let it. It's the plant that Circe used when she turned Ulysses' sailors into pigs and ate them.'

'It must be powerful stuff.'

'It's also said to be an aphrodisiac for men, but I wouldn't know about that.'

He smiled. 'Something in its favour, after all.'

'And in medieval times, people used to believe it protected them from the spells of elves.'

'I don't believe in elves.'

'Nor do I.'

'How about fairies?'

'Never seen them in the garden. I always hoped I would, as a child, but no luck.'

'You had a happy childhood?'

'Idyllic. How about you?'

He thought of the safe and untroubled years in the house in North London. 'Yes. I was very lucky.'

Had Rory Heathcote been as lucky – with everything that money could buy? He didn't think so. The most important things in life – the things that really mattered – were not for sale.

Naomi took another swig from her glass. 'Jacob saw to the grass for you.'

'Yes, I've settled up with him.'

'I unlocked the shed, so he could get at the mower. You've got it all organized in there, haven't you, Hugh? Everything in its place.

'That's the way I like it.'

He had already hidden the key elsewhere. Where she'd never find it.

She shook her head and the flowers and the feathers all quivered beneath the veil.

'I'll never understand men and their sheds.'

'You don't need to, Naomi,' he said.

When Naomi had left, the Colonel climbed up into the loft. This involved a certain amount

180

of wrestling with a collapsible ladder and an uncooperative trap door. Once up there, he switched on his torch. Here were the suitcases, and the cardboard boxes and the tin trunk that he had stowed away out of sight and mind when he had moved into the cottage. In the trunk he found some blankets that he thought might be useful for Freda Butler's Homeless cause and, opening a crocodile-skin suitcase acquired during an Africa posting many years ago, he came across the British Warm coat that he used to wear when he was home on leave in England. He added it to the blankets. A visit to Boots in Dorchester would deal with the shampoo, toothpaste and soap that had been requested.

He shone the torch into corners and, close by the cold water tank, he saw what he had been searching for: a dry-cleaner's plastic bag with a hanger hook at the top. He hauled it down the ladder, together with the blankets and the British Warm, and carried it into his bedroom.

The plastic bag unzipped and he drew out his old morning suit – the black coat with the tails, the striped trousers, the dove-grey waistcoat. Thirteen years since he had last worn it at Marcus's and Susan's wedding. This, he thought ruefully, was the moment of truth.

He tried on the trousers first, then the waistcoat, and, then, the coat, breathing in as he fastened buttons. The miracle was that the suit still fitted him – a little tighter than before, perhaps, but perfectly wearable. He looked at his reflection in the long glass. The man standing there was older, greyer and no wiser. For the life of him, he couldn't see what Naomi had been on about.

They were lucky with the weather. The sun shone on the morning of the wedding and went on shining all day. The villagers, dressed up in their finery, converged on the church and filled it to standing room only.

The Colonel, a yellow rose in his buttonhole, arrived with the bride in a hired Daimler that had been polished to gleaming perfection. All brides were beautiful, he knew, but it seemed to him that Ruth was the most beautiful that he had seen since Laura. At the church, he helped her from the car and she laid her hand on his arm as they went up the path. At the open west door they paused. Ahead, he could see the packed pews, Tom Harvey and his best man standing at the end of the nave aisle. He had done the same himself once, long ago. He could remember exactly how it had been, waiting for Laura, and the heart-stopping moment when he had turned round to see her coming towards him.

'Ready, Ruth?'

She smiled up at him and nodded. 'Ready'.

The organ wheezed into life, coaxed by the valiant Miss Hartshorne at the keys, and the congregation stood to sing the first hymn, *Praise my Soul, the King of Heaven,* as the Colonel and Ruth walked slowly towards the altar. Smiling faces turned to watch their progress; even the Major managed an approving nod. Among the sea of hats, he caught a glimpse of

Great-Aunt Rosalind's magnificent flower and feather creation, of Mrs Cuthbertson's pink tulle dustbin lid, and of Miss Butler's neat navy straw. He knew most of the smiling faces; and they knew him.

Like his old cat, the Colonel had finally come home.

Lightning Source UK Ltd.
Milton Keynes UK
UKOW02n1338301015

261743UK00001B/3/P